Some Summer!

by Jean Vandevenne

D0595676

Bob Jones University Press, Greenville, South Carolina 29614

Some Summer!

Edited by Olivia Tschappler

Cover and illustrations by Marty Hartman

©1987 Bob Jones University Press
Greenville, South Carolina 29614

ISBN 0-89084-380-5
Printed in the United States of America

20   19   18   17   16   15   14   13   12   11   10   9

To Tom, Liz, Paul, Mary, and Buzz, who each contributed a special kind of inspiration.

Publisher's Note

For an eleven-year-old boy, Charlie Scott has his life pretty well mapped out. He has his hobbies and his interests, and a certain portion of his time has been carefully allotted (by his mother) to church. He is saved, and he has a Christian family, but Charlie has decided that Sunday morning, Sunday evening, and Wednesday night are probably sufficient sacrifices for a normal Christian life.

It takes a whole summer of the cantankerous Aunt Essie and a solid week of Vacation Bible School to teach Charlie the importance of his relationship with God. Gradually Charlie comes to realize that the Lord is dealing with him. Charlie becomes more and more aware of the person of God and how much he needs to be in fellowship with the Lord.

Some Summer! is a light, entertaining novel that elementary students will enjoy. Its message of God's love and guidance is timely and appropriate for children.

Contents

Chapter One
Charlie's Treasure

Charlie Scott leaned against the corner of the garage, every inch of him spelling boredom. The Scotts' beagle-dachshund, Red (of course he wasn't really red, but he was red for a dog), lay limply beside Charlie looking equally bored, his long muzzle resting flat on the cement.

In front of the big garage door, Charlie's brother Ben and their friends Doug and Mike Grandy scuffled good-naturedly under the basketball hoop for possession of the ball.

It was the usual after-school meeting of their gang. It wasn't that other boys weren't welcome to be friends with them; it was just that there weren't any other boys close by, none that were the right age, anyway. Once upon a time Charlie's mother had called them the Freckle Gang, owing to one feature that all four boys had in common. Charlie had the most freckles, which was to be expected because of his red hair. (Well, not red, really, but red for a boy.) Ben, who had dark brown hair, was next, and the Grandy brothers came in third with about an equally small sprinkling each beneath a thatch of light brown hair. Of course, they didn't call *themselves* the Freckle Gang. They didn't call themselves anything because they couldn't agree on a good name.

"Hey, Charlie, aren't you going to play?" somebody called from the scuffle under the basketball hoop.

Charlie, under the spell of the early May sunshine, shrugged. It felt like spring at last, although it had been spring for a long time according to the calendar. And it was Friday. Friday was always special because of two free days ahead. This was a day to do something new and exciting, Charlie thought. They had played basketball most of the winter—whenever the driveway was clear of snow. Basketball was what they played when they couldn't think of anything else to do. Charlie had had enough of basketball.

"I'm going to ride around town," he announced, coming to life at last. He went into the house to sign out on the chalkboard that his mother kept by the back door for that purpose.

Charlie's mother was a nurse. For longer than Charlie could remember, she had worked for Dr. Blake, whose office was just a block down the street. Charlie's father had died when Charlie was a baby, and his mother had gone to work to make a living for the family. For years a succession of sitters ("not *baby*sitters, Mom!" Ben and Charlie always objected) had been hired to keep tabs on the Scott boys. Last fall in a family conference, Ben, Charlie, and their mother had decided that the boys were old enough to keep tabs on themselves, with a few ground rules. One of those rules was signing out on the chalkboard when they left the yard.

This taken care of, Charlie picked up his bike, which had been lying on the grass by the back door. Red, close at his heels, wagged his tail expectantly.

Charlie scooped up Red and stuffed him into the left-hand side of the bike's saddle baskets. That was Red's special place. Not the right-hand side. When Charlie put him on the right-hand side he jumped out, sooner or later—usually sooner. On the left side Red had never been known to jump out, whether the bike was in motion, or parked somewhere waiting for Charlie.

"See you, Charlie," a voice called from the basketball huddle.

Charlie pushed his bike around the back of the garage, across the lawn, and then, hopping on, pedaled down the alley toward town, leaving behind the slap, slap, slap of the ball.

When Charlie rode his bicycle around town, he usually went through the alleys for a reason. It was along the alleys that people set out the things that they wanted to get rid of. Of course, Charlie didn't poke around in just anybody's trash, but most of the neighbors and the storekeepers on Main Street were only too happy for someone to make use of their discards. And if anybody could, it was Charlie. There was no telling what he might find in his rides through the alleys that would make a valuable addition to his culch pile.

Nobody else in MacArthur had a culch pile like Charlie Scott's. In fact, nobody he knew even had one, except Uncle Nate's friend, Mr. Gage, who lived in Winchester, fifteen miles away. That was where Charlie had gotten the idea in the first place.

A culch pile, according to Mr. Gage, was a collection of things somebody else might throw away—odd screws, bolts, nuts, springs, old motors, scraps of wood and metal, handles from broken tools, and the like. But if you had a good enough culch pile, you always had what you needed to build or repair almost anything. Mr. Gage had that kind of culch pile. And Charlie had been working on his own, ever since he had seen Mr. Gage's.

Culch, according to Charlie's mother, was another word for rubbish. She had mentioned this one day at house-cleaning time as she eyed the growing pile in the corner of the basement. However, she rarely complained anymore because when something needed to be fixed around the house, Charlie and the culch pile usually came through.

To Charlie, the really good thing about the culch pile was that when he wanted to make something—even if at first he didn't know what he wanted to make— he always had something to start with.

Charlie had been working on the culch pile for almost a year now. He had found no other hobby nearly so rewarding.

The best thing he had made so far from the things he had collected was a model airplane that he had constructed last year when he was ten. It was like one he had once seen at an air show. It was an old-timer, a biplane with an open cockpit. Charlie had made it from parts of a discarded toy car and some other odds and ends. It even had a miniature pilot with a helmet and goggles like the man had worn who had flown the real airplane at the air show. Charlie's pilot had been the driver of a toy car. The helmet he had made from a worn-out leather mitten, and the goggles he had bent into shape from some wire. Charlie's plane didn't fly, but it had a propeller attached to a long, heavy rubber band, and when he wound it up, the plane shuddered and shook just like the real one when it was getting ready to take off. It had won a blue ribbon at the school hobby fair last month. "Most Original Entry," the ribbon said. Now the plane hung suspended from a heavy wire over the table Ben and Charlie used for a desk in their room.

Pedaling through two blocks of alley without finding anything interesting, Charlie came out on Academy Street. Beyond was MacArthur's business district. Often the trash boxes behind the stores yielded useful finds. Sometimes even Ben, Doug, and Mike left their basketball game to join Charlie in poking around behind the stores.

Charlie hesitated a moment, deciding whether to go straight across Academy or to turn and ride down the alley on the other side of Main Street first. The deciding factor was, did he want to do the best first, or save it until last? The best was Folsom's Hardware—straight ahead.

A hardware store, to Charlie, was a fascinating place full of materials for inventing and building things.

Sometimes in the hardware trash box Charlie found the stuff—only slightly shopworn or with parts missing—that he had dreamed over in the store.

"Best first," Charlie decided aloud. After all, the most interesting place on the other side of the street was George's TV shop, and the culch pile was already overstocked with burned out TV tubes and the like. There was a limit to what anybody could do with that sort of thing.

Behind the barber shop, the first building in the block of stores, Charlie recognized Uncle Nate's blue station wagon.

Uncle Nate was Charlie's mother's brother. "Little brother," Mom called him sometimes, because he was the younger of the two, but she smiled when she said it. In almost any crowd Uncle Nate stood out as the tallest one. He was a bachelor and traveled during the week selling farm machinery. When he made the trip back home to the city on Fridays, he usually stopped in MacArthur to have supper with the Scotts. He must be getting a haircut now, Charlie thought.

He decided to ride around to the front window of the barber shop for a minute to wave at Uncle Nate. He might even go inside. He liked the atmosphere of the barber shop. It was sort of a man's world. And there were vending machines where, for a penny, you could get a handful of peanuts or jellybeans or a jawbreaker. Charlie rarely got to go to the barber shop because his mother usually cut his and Ben's hair herself to save money.

Just as he started to turn up the sidewalk, Charlie saw something that made him forget all about Uncle Nate and the barber shop. Something that could be the makings of the most exciting project he had ever built.

There on the other side of Uncle Nate's car, in back of Folsom's Hardware, was a pile of old lumber. Charlie had heard Mr. Folsom say he was going to have the back partition of the store taken out to make more display space. That must be where the lumber came from.

Hopping off his bike, he pushed the kickstand down and hurried over.

He looked longingly at the pile of lumber. Was it too much to hope that Mr. Folsom was going to throw away all that?

The back door of the hardware store creaked open, and two men wearing carpenters' aprons came out, each with an arm load of wood.

"Hey, sonny!" one of them said as they tossed their loads down with a clatter. "How about a nice pile of lumber today?"

"Sure," Charlie said, trying not to sound too eager. He wasn't certain whether the man was joking or not.

"No fooling, would you like it?" the man asked.

Charlie nodded vigorously. "Yes, sir!" -

"Tell you what. Mr. Folsom wants this cleaned up before tomorrow so's not to have the alley cluttered up for Saturday business. If you'll haul it away today, you can have it. Is it a deal?"

"Deal!"

"Okay, it's yours!" the man said and went back inside, followed by the other carpenter.

Charlie looked over the lumber, scarcely able to believe his good fortune. If he worked it right, what he had in mind would be exciting enough to get the rest of the gang to help him haul the lumber home, and make them forget about playing basketball for a long time.

Charlie was the youngest of the gang at eleven, a year younger than his brother Ben. Mike was Ben's age, and Doug a year older than Ben and Mike. Usually, being the youngest didn't matter, except that when Charlie got an idea for the four of them to work on together, it had to be really good, or they'd end up playing basketball.

Well, this time they wouldn't end up playing basketball, Charlie thought, as he pulled some two-by-fours from the pile. These were just what they needed to build something that they had talked about many times—a clubhouse of their very own!

It had seemed an impossible dream, but now that he had found the materials, Charlie was sure that the four of them together could build it. Although none of them had ever done that kind of building, they had watched when a new house was being built down the street last summer. The two-by-fours were what made the framework. Then you nailed the wider boards onto that, and you had some kind of a building. Of course, there was more to it than that, but that was how you got started, anyway.

"Hey, Charlie!"

Charlie looked up to see Uncle Nate coming around the side of the barber shop. "Hi!" he called. A tall, thin man in a suit and tie was walking with Uncle Nate— Pastor Danford.

Red, wriggling in excitement, gave an enthusiastic woof from his place in the left-hand bicycle basket.

Uncle Nate stopped to give Red a friendly scratch behind the ears and then walked over to Charlie and the pile of lumber. Pastor was already surveying the pile of lumber and Charlie's bike basket with a little smile. He and Uncle Nate looked at each other, then at the lumber, then at Charlie, and shook their heads. "You aren't thinking of adding that to your culch pile, are you?" Uncle Nate asked.

"Well, sort of," Charlie said. "I thought maybe we could build something with it—Ben and Doug and Mike and me. We've been thinking about building a clubhouse for a long time. The carpenters that are working for Mr. Folsom said I could have it if I hauled it away today. I don't think Mom would care, do you?" That question hadn't occurred to him until this minute.

Uncle Nate rubbed his chin, thinking. Pastor picked up a small piece of wood. "Plenty good for building," he observed.

"Mom likes for us to have things to do to keep busy," Charlie continued, "and it wouldn't cost anything. I've got lots of nails and stuff already in my culch pile. We could build it out on the Back Forty."

The Back Forty was an empty lot belonging to the Scotts across the alley from their back yard. It was overgrown with brush and young trees. The boys had played there often before basketball had become their consuming passion. It had been a dandy place for kick-the-can and cowboys and Indians, or for just getting away from the world in general. Charlie never quite understood why it was called the Back Forty, except that Grandpa Scott had called the forty acres of wooded pastureland at the back of his farm by the same name.

Uncle Nate agreed that his sister probably wouldn't have any objections to the idea of the boys building a clubhouse. "If she does, I'll help persuade her," he said. "Why don't I take what lumber I can in my car? I have some business in the country right now, but I'll bring it when I come to your house for supper."

Together the three of them loaded lumber into the back of the station wagon on top of some boxes and display cases that had to do with the farm machinery business. When they had filled all the empty spaces, they had made a good dent in the pile of lumber.

"Well, I think there's just enough room for you if you want a lift home, Pastor," Uncle Nate said when they had finished.

"Thanks, Nate. Say, Charlie, let me know how the work goes," Pastor said. "I'll keep my ears open for news of any other wood that folks'll be getting rid of." Then he got into the car with Uncle Nate.

Charlie yelled his thanks as Uncle Nate drove out of the alley.

"You'll have to walk home," he informed Red as he lifted him from the side bike basket. Red, tail wagging, investigated the pile of lumber while Charlie piled some of the shorter pieces into the baskets.

When they were full, he laid the ends of a couple of two-by-fours on top of the lumber in the baskets, letting the other ends rest on either side of the handlebars. Then he headed up the alley toward home, walking his loaded bike as fast as possible.

Red, apparently not the least offended that he had been ousted from his usual place by a pile of old lumber, trotted along behind.

Chapter Two
A Big Plan

The rest of the gang was still playing basketball. Charlie could hear the ball hitting the cement above the rattle of the lumber as he neared home.

He clattered into the yard from the alley and noisily began to unload the lumber beside the garage. Red danced around him, barking. Then he scrambled around front to announce their return.

The slap of the basketball stopped suddenly, and Mike, Ben, and Doug appeared around the corner of the garage. Doug still clutched the ball.

"Hey, Charlie, where'd you get that?" Ben asked.

"Back of Folsom's."

The other boys looked speculatively at the lumber. Charlie could almost hear wheels turning inside their heads.

"That all there was?" Mike asked.

"Nope," Charlie answered. "There's a whole big pile of it. They're tearing out the back partition in the hardware store."

"That'd be a lot of lumber," Ben said. "Enough to build a clubhouse, maybe."

"I think so," Charlie replied coolly. He had them on his hook now. "If you guys want to help me haul it, we can have it. Uncle Nate's got a bunch of it in his car, but there's lots more, and Mr. Folsom wants it out of the way today."

"Let's go!" Ben, Doug, and Mike agreed.

As Charlie had expected, the other boys were impressed with the possibilities of the pile of lumber behind the hardware store. The four boys worked hard for the rest of the afternoon moving the material by bike and coaster wagon to the Scott's back yard. When the carpenters climbed into their pickup at quitting time, the small gang of boys was headed up the alley with the last load.

The moving job finished, the boys lazed on the pile of lumber—their lumber—and added to the plans that had been flying back and forth between them as they worked. Red flopped down with them, tongue lolling as he surveyed the Back Forty with satisfaction.

A tree house was what they really wanted, but there weren't any trees big enough for a tree house on the Back Forty.

"Maybe we could build it up on stilts," Charlie said in a sudden flash of inspiration. "The two-by-fours are plenty long enough, don't you think?"

"Yeah!" Ben agreed excitedly. "And we could put a trap door in the floor instead of having a regular door;

so when anybody walked up to it, he couldn't see the door."

"Good idea!" Doug said.

"That might be almost as good as a tree house," Mike added.

Charlie could picture it all in his mind already. The clubhouse on stilts. A secret entrance. And, of course, there'd be all the fun of building it. They could have camp outs in it sometimes. Probably they'd hardly play basketball all summer, they'd be so busy with the clubhouse, building it, and having fun in it after they got it built. This was going to be some summer!

Two short honks of a car horn announced Uncle Nate's arrival. He always sounded it a certain way, and Charlie thought he would recognize Uncle Nate's honk anywhere. The boys raced to the driveway to unload the rest of their lumber.

Charlie's mother had evidently been home for a while, for near the open back door the promising aroma of supper was in the air. In a few minutes she stepped to the door to announce that the meal was ready.

Friday night supper was always special because of Uncle Nate's being there. It was a Friday evening custom, like going to church on Sunday. It felt good, somehow, to have a man in the house. Charlie didn't remember his father, so he couldn't really say he missed him, but having Uncle Nate around helped to fill a space that needed filling in Charlie's life.

At the table Uncle Nate asked the blessing—a rather lengthy one, as usual—including loved ones nearby, extending to the needy in foreign lands, and finally ending with the food at hand. When Uncle Nate got to talking to God, time sort of got away from him, but Charlie could forgive him for that.

Having finally arrived at the amen, Ben and Charlie loaded their plates with generous helpings of meat loaf and mashed potatoes and lesser portions of the green beans and lettuce salad. For once, though, their minds were not on eating. Interrupting each other from one sentence to the next, they told their mother about the lumber and what they planned to do with it.

"Can we, Mom?" both boys asked together.

She laughed. "*May* we, if you're asking my permission, though it sounds as if the clubhouse is already as good as built. What do you think, Nate?"

Uncle Nate shrugged. "What's the harm?" he said, winking at Charlie. "They got the materials for nothing, and they have a good place to build it. It could be a valuable experience for them."

"I suppose so," Mom said slowly, nodding. "All right boys, you have my permission. Just keep the mess out on the Back Forty. And be careful. I don't want you getting hurt. Now you'd better eat before everything gets cold."

Man, am I tired, Charlie thought as he attacked his mountain of mashed potatoes. They had worked hard to get all that lumber out of the alley. It was a good thing he'd decided to ride down there instead of hanging around shooting baskets with the other guys.

Back and forth, from one end of the table to the other, his mother's and Uncle Nate's conversation bounced. It was like a Ping-Pong ball, Charlie thought absently, not really paying attention to what they were saying. He and Ben were the clamps that held the net on each side of the table. Mom sent her conversational Ping-Pong ball over to Uncle Nate, and he returned it. Then Mom sent it back. Back and forth and back and forth.

Then the Ping-Pong ball hit the net.

"You boys don't remember Aunt Essie, do you?" Mom was asking.

Aunt Essie? With effort Charlie focused in on the conversation.

"Is she the one who lives in Florida and sends a basket of oranges and grapefruit at Christmas time and used to own our house?" Ben asked.

"Yes, that's Aunt Essie," Mom said.

That was funny, Charlie thought. Usually when he thought of a person, a face came to his mind, but when he heard the name Aunt Essie, he always pictured a basket of oranges and grapefruit.

Aunt Essie, he knew, was his mother's aunt—and Uncle Nate's, too, of course. When her husband, Uncle Henry, died, Aunt Essie had sold the house to the Scotts and had moved to Florida. That was before Ben and Charlie could remember.

"Aunt Essie's coming to spend the summer with us," Mom announced. "We got a letter from her today."

Charlie tried to replace the basket of oranges and grapefruit with the image of an elderly lady. She would sit in the rocking chair in the living room and knit, he supposed. That was what Grandma Scott did. Or she would peel potatoes for his mother in the kitchen. Grandma Scott and the other aunts always did that when they came for a visit.

Nobody had ever come to stay a whole summer before, but Charlie guessed it would be all right. Anyway, he and Ben would be busy building the clubhouse on the Back Forty. What did it matter who came for a visit or how long she stayed?

Chapter Three
Aunt Essie

The day was just like summer. A perfect day for clubhouse construction, Charlie thought as he elbowed his way out of the school building at three fifteen. A whole week had passed since he had found the lumber for the clubhouse. The pile still stood beside the garage. It had rained most of the week. On one day it hadn't rained, but he and Ben had gone to the dentist. At last, though, it was Friday. The day was clear, and nobody had to go anywhere. This afternoon they could finally start on the clubhouse.

Impatiently, Charlie waited for Ben and Mike by the bike rack outside the school building. Doug, being in the seventh grade, rode the bus to the junior high school in Hamilton and wouldn't be home until later.

Ben and Mike were taking a long time, it seemed to Charlie. Probably their whole class was having to stay in late for being noisy. Why couldn't people just keep quiet and avoid trouble—especially on Fridays when the whole weekend was waiting, just waiting outside the double doors?

Charlie backed his bike away from the rack. He swung a leg over and settled himself on the seat, rolling the bike slightly backward and forward with his feet, his hands twisting on the handlebars.

He had half a mind to go on ahead by himself, but just as he was about to give himself a forward push, the sixth graders came swarming out the double doors.

Ben and Mike wheeled out their bikes, and the three boys headed for the Scotts' house.

They were just going up the alley behind Dr. Blake's when Mrs. Scott called to them from the back door of the office.

Ben and Charlie groaned. She probably had something for them to do, though they had hurried to finish their daily chores that morning so they could have the whole time after school to work on the clubhouse.

"I'm sorry," she said as the boys rode into the gravel parking lot to see what she wanted, "but I'm afraid I'll have to ask you boys to go down to meet Aunt Essie's bus. An emergency root canal has come up, and I can't get away for a little while yet."

Aunt Essie. Charlie had forgotten all about her.

"I'm really sorry," Mom repeated. "I know you were planning to start on your clubhouse, but this shouldn't take long. You'll have to go right away, though. The bus is due in a few minutes. Leave any heavy luggage she has for Uncle Nate to pick up later."

It was no use to argue. Somebody had to meet Aunt Essie.

"I'll come over later," Mike said, sounding a little disappointed, and rode off.

Ben and Charlie started toward the front of the doctor's office and Main Street with their bikes, but their mother reminded them that it wouldn't be very gracious of them to ride their bikes while Aunt Essie walked home. So they took their bikes home and set off toward town on foot. It wasn't that far to walk— less than three blocks. It was just that they preferred to go by wheels rather than by feet. Red tagged along with them, veering off every now and then to nose around for interesting smells.

There was not a regular bus station in the town. MacArthur was too small for that. The bus stopped at the drugstore. There was a bench inside the store where people could wait for the bus. Usually, though, anybody who had much of a wait sat at the soda fountain with a soft drink or coffee and talked to Mr. Benson who had owned the drugstore for much longer than the boys could remember.

"What if a bunch of people get off the bus?" Ben wondered grumpily on the way to town. "How will we know which one is Aunt Essie?"

"We'll stand there and holler 'Aunt Essie' until she answers," Charlie said recklessly. He knew, of course, that neither of them would do that. He was suddenly in what his mother called a slaphappy mood. He sometimes got that way when he felt uncomfortable about something. That something right now was having to meet a strange grown-up.

Ben snorted, catching Charlie's mood. "No, we'll look for a basket of grapefruit and oranges. That'll be Aunt Essie."

Both boys howled with laughter. The night they had learned of Aunt Essie's visit, Charlie had told Ben about the picture that came to his mind when he heard her name. It hadn't been that funny then, but today—in the slaphappy mood—it was a side-splitting joke.

The bus hadn't yet arrived when they reached the drugstore. The boys explained their errand to Mr. Benson, who had come to the doorway.

"I heard Essie Morgan was coming for a visit," he said. "I knew her years ago. She'll keep things lively around your house," he added in such a way that the boys weren't quite sure whether knowing Aunt Essie was good or bad. Without another word he went back inside.

Before they could decide just what Mr. Benson meant, the bus pulled up. There was a slow hiss of air brakes. Ben and Charlie shifted their feet in expectation.

The bus stood there, motor idling, smelly gas fumes choking MacArthur's main corner, while the driver opened the door and stepped out. There seemed to be only one passenger, an elderly woman, getting off the bus. That must be Aunt Essie. A tall, slender, energetic-appearing person, she spoke to the driver who was taking some suitcases from the luggage compartment. Then, without even looking in the boys' direction, she strode into the drugstore. The driver followed with the luggage.

Ben and Charlie stood on the sidewalk a moment looking at each other blankly, then shrugged and followed the driver inside. Red plopped down outside to wait for them.

Aunt Essie and Mr. Benson were shaking hands and talking like long-lost friends when the boys came back into the store. Mr. Benson motioned to them.

"Here's a couple of young men come to meet you, Essie. Guess you didn't see them out on the sidewalk," he said.

"Why, it's Lucy's boys, isn't it!" Aunt Essie exclaimed, solemnly shaking hands with Ben and Charlie.

Ben explained stiffly to Aunt Essie why their mother hadn't been able to meet the bus.

"Well, that's just all right," Aunt Essie said. "I don't want to be a bother to anybody."

They left the largest of Aunt Essie's suitcases for Uncle Nate to pick up later and started for home. Ben carried two small suitcases and Charlie a medium-sized one. Aunt Essie strode along carrying a cloth shopping bag with a picture of a palm tree on it, and her purse, which resembled a small suitcase. She didn't speak to them again, and Charlie wondered if she had forgotten about them.

Though the luggage wasn't really heavy, the boys were puffing by the time they reached home. Aunt Essie didn't walk like any old lady they had known before. They could just as well have ridden their bikes, Charlie thought. Aunt Essie wouldn't have had any trouble

keeping up. And it would have been easier to carry the suitcases.

Fortunately, Mom had arrived home just ahead of them, so the boys were saved from having to entertain Aunt Essie. Relieved, they rushed upstairs to their room to change their clothes.

Chapter Four
Bad News

When Ben and Charlie came downstairs, their mother was in the kitchen fixing a tray with a pot of tea and a plate of fancy little cookies.

"There's some milk and cookies for you boys on the table," she said.

That was good. Charlie was hoping that they weren't expected to come to a tea party. He and Ben didn't care for tea, and the cookies were too small to be any fun to eat politely. They tasted good, but each one was just about enough for one bite, and his mother didn't think that was a good way to eat them. When you didn't have to worry about manners, you could take a whole handful and enjoy them.

The boys finished their snack just as Mike and Doug rolled into the driveway on their bikes. Now, at long last, they could begin to work on the clubhouse.

The first thing was to get the lumber out to the Back Forty. Charlie went to the garage to get the wagon. In the back corner of the garage lay the basketball where it had been left a week ago. That was a good place for it. It could stay there the whole summer for all Charlie cared. Building a clubhouse was going to be more fun than playing basketball.

Piling on as many two-by-fours as the wagon could carry, the boys pulled it out to the Back Forty. Red leaped on top, rode along uncertainly for a few feet, then jumped off again.

"Now, where do you guys think is the best place to build our clubhouse?" Ben asked, looking around the wooded lot.

"Sure don't want it here by the alley," Doug said. "Everybody in town would come snooping around."

"Man, I wish there was a tree big enough so we could build a tree house," Mike said, eyeing the young and rather spindling trees.

"Well, you can't build a tree house in any of these little trees," Ben said, "unless you're going to turn us all into one-pound midgets."

"If we could just move that big maple in front of our house over here," Mike said dreamily. It was hard to give up the idea of a tree house.

"Come on, Mike, we can't build a tree house, and that's that," Doug said.

They finally settled on a spot at the back of the lot. There was a level clearing there, and then the ground sloped down to a woven wire fence lined with bushes. Beyond that there was nothing but open fields, ploughed now, ready for planting. With the leaves out on all the trees and bushes, it would seem quite isolated.

When the boys came back for another load of lumber, Mom and Aunt Essie were walking around the yard looking at the brightly blooming spring flowers.

That was what old ladies liked to do, Charlie thought—walk around looking at flowers in people's yards. He remembered that Grandma Scott never seemed to think a visit was complete without a walk around the yard to look at the flowers. Not that they had many. His mother was too busy working at Dr. Blake's office and keeping house to have time to work in the yard. But there were some things that seemed to come up by themselves, or at least without much help.

Uncle Nate arrived—announced by his famous two honks—just as the boys had dumped the last load of lumber at the site of the clubhouse. Then it was time for supper.

As the adults carried on a lively conversation, Charlie savored the ham, a rare treat in honor of Aunt Essie's arrival, and baked potato. Now and then he sandwiched in a bite of coleslaw, peas, or applesauce.

Dessert tonight, Charlie knew, was banana cream pie. He loved banana cream pie; but then, he liked every kind of pie he had ever eaten. He would have been hard put to have to choose any one kind for a favorite.

Charlie was thinking about pie and enjoying a second generous-sized baked potato smothered in butter and speckled with salt and pepper, when the bombshell dropped that promised to ruin his whole summer.

Somehow in the reverie about pie, he had missed the first part of the conversation, but when he got tuned in, Aunt Essie was saying something about planting a garden in the back yard.

"Oh, Aunt Essie," Mom objected, "you're here for a vacation. I'm not going to let you slave all summer in the hot sun gardening for us! It's kind of you to offer, but we just couldn't let you do that. If I had time to help, that would be different, but much as I would like to, I just don't have time for gardening."

"Aunt Essie, you're not as young as you were thirty years ago," Uncle Nate teased. "What would the neighbors think, our poor old aunt working like that!"

"Humph!" Aunt Essie sniffed indignantly. "Poor old aunt indeed! I may be seventy-three-going-on-seventy-four, but I'm just as strong as I was thirty years ago. Stronger! Besides, Lucy's got two boys here to help. Do them good to learn how to make a garden. Give them something to do this summer, too. Young folks nowadays don't have enough to do. 'Idle hands are the devil's tools,' I always say."

Charlie got a sick feeling in the pit of his stomach. Something to do this summer! That was no problem. He and Ben didn't need any help to keep busy. Their mother did a good enough job of thinking up chores for them to do. This summer they needed what time they had after helping around the house to work on the clubhouse.

Charlie expected his mother to say something about the clubhouse, but she didn't. Instead, she and Uncle Nate started talking about summers long ago and raising gardens and canning things and Aunt Essie's recipes.

Charlie's eyes met Ben's across the table. Both of them knew they couldn't just tell Aunt Essie they didn't want to help her or that they had other things to do. Charlie was irked. She hadn't even asked them anything at all about their plans for the summer before insisting that they would be idle without her garden.

By bedtime that night it was settled. Aunt Essie would plant a garden in the back yard this summer. Mr. Foley was coming in the morning with his tractor to get the ground ready. And—what a revolting development!— Ben and Charlie had been appointed Aunt Essie's helpers for planting, weeding, watering, and harvesting.

Having in one short evening ruined a whole summer, Aunt Essie sat in the rocking chair in the living room watching the news on the television and visiting with Mom and Uncle Nate. She still hadn't spoken as many as ten words to Ben or Charlie, yet she expected them to help her. And nobody had even mentioned the clubhouse to her or all their plans.

The boys clumped up the stairs to bed with long faces.

"I liked her better when she was a basket of grapefruit and oranges," Ben muttered when they had reached the top of the stairs.

"Me too," Charlie said.

Chapter Five
Saturday

Charlie woke the next morning to the roar of Mr. Foley's tractor in the back yard. He lay in bed feeling like two different people. First, there was the Charlie who wanted to hop out of bed, hurry and eat breakfast and get out to the Back Forty to work on the clubhouse. Then there was the other Charlie who, with his brother Ben, had been sentenced to slave labor in Aunt Essie's garden. From what he had seen of Aunt Essie, Charlie had a feeling that the first Charlie with plans for building a clubhouse didn't have a chance.

He rolled over, pulled the covers up over his head, and tried to go back to sleep until the aroma of frying sausage wafted up the stairs and under the covers. Sausage usually meant pancakes for breakfast, especially if it was Saturday. And it was Saturday. Aunt Essie surely wouldn't start a garden on Saturday. She'd want to rest after her trip. Besides, they didn't have anything to plant. Charlie guessed it would be safe to get up after all.

Kicking off the covers, he reached over with his foot to joggle Ben's bed. "Wake up, lazy bones," he said, "we've got things to do!"

Charlie was right about pancakes and sausage for breakfast, but that was all. As soon as the meal was finished, he and Ben found themselves heading toward town with their wagon and Aunt Essie on a seed-and-plant-buying expedition. Charlie wondered if there was any way to win with Aunt Essie. She always seemed to be two jumps ahead of everybody. When she made up her mind about something, it was as good as done. And she still didn't really talk to them, except to tell them to bring their wagon to carry her purchases home. And they didn't feel comfortable talking to each other much when she was near them. It was pretty obvious that she thought children were best seen and not heard.

At Hatcher's Farm and Garden store, Aunt Essie set about making her own selection of seeds and plants. The boys leaned on the front counter watching from a distance.

"Wish she'd buy some watermelon seeds," Charlie said, breaking their silence. "It might not be so bad helping in the garden if we could grow watermelon."

"Yeah," Ben agreed dully. Then he brightened as he looked toward the street. "Hey, there's Doug and Mike! I think they're looking for us."

Ben and Charlie hurried out to the sidewalk.

"Hey, you guys," Doug said excitedly as he and Mike stopped their bikes in front of the store, "we know where there's a bunch of good stuff for the clubhouse!"

"Where?" Ben and Charlie asked together.

"Right next door to us—at the Hutchinsons'," Mike said. "They're remodeling their house. There's some stuff they don't want, and they said we can look it over and have anything we can use."

"Neat!" Charlie exclaimed, ready to go. Then he remembered that things had changed since they had seen Doug and Mike the day before. He and Ben looked at each other hopelessly.

"What's the matter with you guys?" Doug asked.

"We gotta *work* this summer," Ben explained bitterly in a low voice. "All summer long! Aunt Essie got this dumb idea to have a garden in our back yard, and we have to help. She's in there now buying stuff to plant." He nodded toward the store.

"Vegetables and stuff like that," Charlie added disgustedly, "and we have to haul it home."

"Man!" Mike said heavily.

"Don't have to work *all* day, do you?" Doug asked.

"Who knows?" Ben shrugged.

"Maybe when we get the stuff home, we can get away," Charlie suggested.

"Maybe," Ben said doubtfully.

"How long do you think that will be?" Doug asked.

"Maybe a half-hour," Ben said.

"How about coming over to our house then?" Doug said. "Bring your wagon. Come on, Mike, we'll go right now and start sorting out what we want."

Charlie felt torn to pieces inside. Here was a whole bunch of good junk, and he couldn't even get to go and look at it. He didn't want to have to wait a half-hour. He wanted to go right now. And there was a possibility that he might not even get to look at it at all. Not if Aunt Essie had it in her head to plant the garden. He knew now that she was not one to be sitting around resting.

Their business finally finished at Hatcher's, Ben and Charlie trudged along home behind Aunt Essie. Charlie pulled the wagon, now loaded with low cardboard boxes of plants, and Ben carried a brown paper bag of garden seeds. Every now and then she would say something—supposedly to them, Charlie guessed. She might look at a store window in passing and say, "My! Ladies' shoes are on sale today," or "The bank won't be open until Monday—I suppose people don't bother with their accounts on a Saturday." It was always a comment that might interest an old lady, but never anything that boys knew much about. And from the way she walked slightly ahead of them, her eyes roving the shops and the sidewalk, it was clear that she really didn't expect them to answer her or talk.

It would take several trips back to Hatcher's to get all the plants home that Aunt Essie had bought. Who was going to eat all those vegetables, Charlie didn't know, but he hoped that he wouldn't.

And there wasn't a watermelon seed in the lot. The soil wasn't right for melons, Aunt Essie had said—curtly enough—when Charlie had bravely suggested growing some. So that was that.

When they arrived home after the last load, Aunt Essie was nowhere in sight. It would be stupid to ask if they were needed any more, Ben and Charlie decided. They would just go.

Quickly they unloaded the last of the flats of plants beside the garage, signed out, and headed down the driveway with the empty wagon just as Doug and Mike came along.

They weren't quick enough, however.

"Boys," Aunt Essie called from the front door, "don't go away now. I want to get those plants in before they have a chance to wilt. It's already late to plant a garden, so we'll have to get busy."

Charlie was tempted to walk on along as though he hadn't heard, but he knew there'd be trouble when his mother found out. Instead, he stopped, too angry and frustrated to even say anything.

Ben let out an exasperated sigh and called back over his shoulder, "Yes, ma'am," in what might have passed for a polite tone, had Charlie not known that Ben felt exactly as he did.

"Where've you guys been?" Doug wanted to know as he and Mike came to a stop.

"Just back and forth to town about sixteen times for Aunt Essie's dumb plants," Ben answered in disgust, "and now we have to help her plant 'em!"

"Is there any good stuff at the Hutchinsons'?" Charlie asked, almost hoping that there wasn't, since he wouldn't be able to see for himself.

"There sure is!" Mike answered. "How about if Doug and I take your wagon and get what looks good? I think they're about ready to haul it away. We'd better get what we want now."

Ben and Charlie figured that was the only thing they could do under the circumstances. Doug and Mike parked their bikes in the Scotts' driveway and set off toward the Hutchinsons' with the wagon. As though anxious to stay out of Aunt Essie's way himself, Red tagged along after them.

Reluctantly Ben and Charlie followed Aunt Essie to the garage for the wheelbarrow and gardening tools that Aunt Essie said she herself had used years ago when she had owned the Scotts' house.

Looking over the enormous rectangle of newly worked ground that was to be the garden, Aunt Essie crumbled a handful of soil. "Should have been worked over weeks ago, or, better still, last fall," she mused, once again talking but not really wanting them to answer or ask her questions. "But this will have to do. Let's get to work!"

Charlie felt like sitting down and refusing to budge. He had done enough work already. He wanted to go and look over the pile of material at Hutchinsons' himself. This garden was Aunt Essie's idea. Why should he and Ben have to work in it? They had more important things to do.

But there didn't seem to be any way to get out of it. Not without getting into a pack of trouble. Maybe if they got busy and worked fast enough, they could get the garden planted and still have time to work on the clubhouse. Ben seemed to have come to the same conclusion. His feet had been dragging, too, and he'd had a stubborn look on his face, but now he was coming to life.

Aunt Essie broke out of her private musings long enough to show the boys how to use the row marker they had found in the garage. Uncle Henry had made the row marker years ago, she said. It was a wood frame that reminded Charlie of an old-fashioned sled, except that it had four runners instead of two. When it was pulled by its rope handle across the newly prepared garden, the runners left evenly spaced lines.

Like a couple of horses pulling a racing chariot, Ben and Charlie went back and forth from one side of the garden to the other pulling the marker. A couple of times Aunt Essie called a halt, and they had to do a rerun because they had gone crooked. Soon, however, the whole garden was marked off in orderly lines ready for planting.

It was kind of neat, Charlie thought. If he hadn't been in a hurry to finish so they could work on the clubhouse, it could have been fun. The marker reminded him of the line-maker his first grade teacher had used on the chalkboard for teaching printing. He'd always wished he could get his hands on it. It would have been fun to make lines all over the chalkboard. Not just horizontal lines, but vertical ones, too, to make a checkerboard pattern. Or wavy lines, or crisscross ones. But he'd never got the chance. The teacher had always kept the line-maker in a desk drawer so nobody else could use it.

They had just finished setting out the tomato plants when Doug and Mike came rattling across the yard with a wagonload of materials from the Hutchinsons'.

"Look at all the stuff we got!" Mike called.

The wagon was so loaded, it was hard to see just what they had, but Charlie's hands fairly itched to get into it. He could see shiny pieces of formica, fancy wood moldings, some good-sized pieces of plywood, and even some scraps of carpeting.

"Boy, that'll be good!" he exclaimed. "Is there any more?"

"No, we picked out all the good stuff. They've taken the rest to the dump anyway," Doug said, and he and Mike headed for the Back Forty to unload their prizes.

Chapter Six
The Projects Begin

It was past the middle of the afternoon by the time all the plants and seeds had been put into their proper places in the garden.

"That's a good job well done!" Aunt Essie said triumphantly. "Now it can rain tonight."

It wouldn't dare not to, Charlie thought. Not when Aunt Essie was planning on it.

Doug and Mike had been dropping in at regular intervals all day to see if they were finished; so it was not surprising that they came riding into the yard again just as Ben and Charlie were putting away the garden tools.

"Ben and Charlie," Mom called from the kitchen window, "you'd better come in and rest a little. You've been working pretty hard. I'll set out some milk and cookies for you—Doug and Mike, too," she added.

That sounded good to Charlie. It seemed like a long time since lunch, and they had been working hard. He hadn't thought his mother had noticed. Why did she let Aunt Essie be such a slave driver, then? Could it be that even Mom was a little afraid of speaking out to Aunt Essie?

The boys sat around the kitchen table and ate the cookies and milk without saying anything. Ben, with both elbows on the table, rested his chin on one hand and munched a cookie wearily. Even Mike and Doug looked droopy. Charlie guessed they were tired from waiting.

When they had their fill of cookies and milk, they all began to perk up.

"Let's get our tools and stuff," Ben said, pushing his chair back with a scrape. Three other chairs scraped back, and the four boys thumped down the basement stairs. Red joined them out back and pranced among them, ears flapping.

Ben and Charlie collected two hammers and an old saw from the workbench that had been their father's. The saw was rusty and not very sharp, but at least it was a saw.

With the other boys looking over his shoulder, Charlie rummaged around in the boxes that held his culch pile. Ah, there it was—a coffee can full of nails that he had been collecting. And there was the folding ruler he had found just the other day in the trash behind Folsom's Hardware. It had been an eight-foot one, but part of it was broken off, so now it measured just six feet two inches, but it was usable, in case they needed to measure something.

Then Charlie thought of something else, a tarpaulin he had found in the trash box behind Hatcher's Farm and Garden Store. It had a hole in one corner, but otherwise it was in good condition.

"We can use this to put over our lumber and stuff in case it rains," he said.

The pile of lumber, together with the newly acquired materials from the Hutchinsons', lay in the clearing on the Back Forty just begging to be made into a clubhouse. Charlie couldn't help feeling excited.

Now that they were there, though, all ready with the tools and everything, the boys looked first at the pile of material and then at each other.

The problem was how to begin.

It was one thing to watch carpenters build a house. Building something yourself was quite different.

"The two-by-fours . . . ," Charlie began uncertainly, half to himself. And then slowly the idea of how to begin came to him.

"We plant the ends of four two-by-fours—one for each corner—in the ground. That'll be the stilts. And then a little way up—just high enough to crawl under— we nail on more two-by-fours all around in a square to fasten the floor boards to."

The other boys thought that would do for a start.

Then Charlie had another inspiration. "I know just the thing we need to dig holes. I'll be right back." He took off running for the garage.

He had seen this interesting-looking shovel when they were gathering tools for making the garden this morning.

Funny, it had been there in the garage all those years, and he had never noticed it. Probably that was because he'd never paid any attention to the gardening tools. It was two small rounded shovels facing each other and fastened to each other with a long bolt to make a hinge. A post-hole digger, Aunt Essie had called it while rummaging through the garage and talking to herself.

It took a little experimenting to find out how to work the post-hole digger. You had to raise it high, Charlie discovered, to bring it down with enough force to make it bite the ground. Once it was in the ground, you pulled the handles apart to make the shovels come together, gathering up the loose earth. When you pulled the digger up, there was the start of a nice, round hole. Then you crossed the handles in the other direction and emptied the shovels.

Thump! Charlie shoved the digger into the ground. Scritch-creak! The digger protested as he pulled the handles apart. Huuumph! Charlie lifted the digger from the ground. Scritch-creak-plop! He crossed the handles and opened them the other direction, and the loose dirt fell out.

"Neat!" the others admired the handiwork of Charlie and the post-hole digger.

"Yeah, and hard work!" Charlie informed them. After digging only a few shovels full, his upper arms ached, and he was only too happy to let the others have a turn at the wonderful tool.

Thump! Scritch-creak! Huuuumph! Scritch-creak-plop!

One by one, four holes were dug and the two-by-fours lowered into place. The boys kicked the loose earth around the two-by-fours and stomped it hard to make them stand firm and straight.

Charlie was so tired by the time that was done that he was glad to hear the ring of the little hand bell his mother used to call them when they were a distance from the house. He thought he had just about enough strength left to make it to the house for supper.

Chapter Seven
Early Progress

A curious thing happened on Sunday morning. Charlie could hear his mother's voice from far away, calling him. Something kept rocking him a little bit, forcing him up from under waves and waves of sleep. Annoyed, he opened his eyes and saw that his mother was standing over him, shaking his shoulder.

"What's—what's the matter, Mom?" he asked.

"It's time to get up, Charlie."

He didn't believe it at first. She bent over Ben and woke him up, too. Sunlight streamed into the room. Outside the window, birds called back and forth.

"It really is morning," he said, and got up on his elbows. Then he groaned. His arms and shoulders ached.

Next to him, Ben moaned. "Oh Mom, do we *have* to get up?"

"You boys overdid it yesterday," she told them. "I can't even remember the last time I had to get you out of bed."

"Breakfast!" Aunt Essie's voice called. Mom was already going out the door, and Charlie allowed himself the luxury of a groan at Aunt Essie.

He was sleepy all through Sunday School, and in church he would have leaned his head against his mother's shoulder except that Aunt Essie was sitting on his other side, and every time he moved she fixed him with a disapproving frown.

After church, on the way out the door, Pastor shook hands with him and said, "Well, Charlie, how's the clubhouse going?"

"Oh, pretty good," he began. "We did have a few problems getting it started, but then I got an idea." He was just about to explain about the stilts when behind him Aunt Essie said, "Oh, my, Pastor Danford, you preach so much like your father!" And Pastor turned to her. Somehow Charlie found himself out the door. Ben, who had been just ahead of him, said, "Aunt Essie knows how to keep a line moving."

Charlie could feel his ears burning. He hadn't finished talking to Pastor! Without a word to Ben or anybody else, he went down the few steps to the parking lot. He wished that Aunt Essie would go back to Florida.

Ben came down after him. "Don't worry, you can tell Pastor about it tonight. Maybe he'd like to come see it soon. He might come with Uncle Nate."

That made Charlie feel better. He knew that Pastor Danford liked him, and he also knew that when a little old lady interrupted someone it was still good manners to listen to her. Pastor Danford had to be polite. Charlie sighed and jammed his hands into his pockets. "Well, this summer can't last forever," he said.

"I hope not," Ben agreed.

On Monday after school Ben and Charlie crossed the yard past the garden that could hold no claim on them for at least a few days. There was one good thing about having just planted a garden, Charlie decided. You didn't have to do anything about it for a while except wait for it to grow. He was in no hurry for that.

It had rained quite obligingly Saturday night, and the plants stood as straight and green in their rows as though they had been there for weeks. But the boys had definitely not come out to look at the garden. They were just passing by on their way to the Back Forty. Red, happy to have Ben and Charlie freed again, ran circles around the boys as they walked along to the Back Forty.

The two-by-fours that were the beginning of the clubhouse stood tall and fairly straight, waiting for the next step in construction.

"Let's pick out some two-by-fours to nail around the ones that are stuck in the ground," Charlie said, rummaging through the lumber pile. He pulled out one that looked suitable. While he and Ben were deciding how high to nail it, Doug and Mike arrived, hammers in hand. Red padded forward to greet them, then returned, leading the way.

The floor needed to be just high enough so they could crawl under it comfortably to get to the trap door, they all decided. Doug, the tallest, got down on his hands and knees, and Charlie measured with his ruler.

Twenty-eight inches was about the right height. With Charlie holding the ruler against each upright, Mike scratched a line with a nail to mark the place for nailing. They had learned that trick watching the carpenters work.

"This is too long," Doug observed, holding the two-by-four between two of the uprights.

"Then we'll have to saw it off," Ben said, "but maybe it would be easier to saw after we nail it on."

When they had nailed the two-by-four in place, Ben picked up the saw. "I'll cut this end off, and you guys can pick out some more two-by-fours," he said.

Charlie, Doug, and Mike quickly found the necessary two-by-fours. Ben's sawing, however, was not so easily taken care of.

"This is work!" he said, his face flushed, sweat running off his forehead. "This wood is hard as a rock!"

"Here, let me do it," Doug said, and sawed away until he, too, had worked up a sweat, but still had not cut through the wood. "This saw is dull," he decided.

Charlie and Mike each took a turn, and then Ben took his second time around. At last the saw chewed its way through the last bit of wood and the too-long piece fell to the ground with a thud.

"There's gotta be a better way than this," Ben declared, ducking his head to wipe his dripping face on the sleeve of his T-shirt.

"Yeah," Doug agreed. "We'll never get the thing built at this rate."

"That's for sure," Mike muttered.

Charlie was silent. He was having an idea.

"Hey," he said after a moment, "why saw the rest of the boards off? We can just let the ends stick out. "Look!" To demonstrate, Charlie laid three two-by-fours out on the ground around the uprights.

"Yeah!" he continued, his idea getting better all the time. "Then we can let the floorboards stick out like that, too, and we'll have a porch. We won't have to do any sawing at all, at least not for a while."

"I'm all for that!" Doug said fervently.

"Me, too!" Mike said.

"Good idea!" Ben added, giving Charlie a brotherly slap on the back.

They had begun to nail on the floorboards, when suddenly they remembered that they had forgotten something. Something very important. The trap door!

"What a bunch of dumb bunnies!" Mike said, slapping his hand to his forehead.

The problem was, they couldn't simply lay the floor and then cut out the door in midair to make an opening, even if they wanted to do all that sawing. There had to be something to nail the frame of the door to, to hold them up around the open space.

Doug, Mike, and Ben all looked at Charlie as though they expected him to come up with the solution.

Charlie was glad to hear the bell calling them to supper just then. One bright idea in an afternoon was about all he could come up with after a hard day at school. He'd have to think about the trap-door opening.

After supper, their homework done, more or less, Ben and Charlie sat at the table-desk in their room under the shadow of Charlie's model plane. Together they brainstormed on the trap door problem.

There was only one solution, as far as they could see. That is, a solution that didn't involve sawing. It wasn't entirely satisfactory, but it would have to do, unless somebody—namely Doug or Mike—had a better idea. Nobody had by the time the gang got together the next day after school.

"If you've got a way figured out so we don't have to do any sawing, let's do it," Doug said.

"The only trouble is, it'll make part of the floor a little higher than the rest," Charlie said.

"Aw, that won't matter," Mike said. "What's your idea?"

"Well," Charlie said, "we nail on more floorboards up to here." He laid a board parallel to the others to mark where they should lay the floorboards lengthwise, until they had an open strip about two feet wide along one side of the clubhouse. Then he took another board and laid it across the gap and perpendicular to the other floorboards, making a square frame at one corner of the clubhouse. Carefully, he sat down on the frame, swung his feet over the opening and crawled out underneath. "That's about the right size, I think," he said, straightening up again.

"Then for this strip of empty space we just nail more boards on crosswise all the rest of the way back," Ben finished explaining the plan. "The cross boards will overlap the long ones, but it can't be helped."

So that was how it happened that part of the floor of the clubhouse was a half-inch higher than the rest, and that there were two porches instead of one, a front porch and a side porch.

When the time came for the trap door itself, Mike remembered a piece of plywood from the scraps he and Doug had scrounged from the Hutchinsons' remodeling project.

He pulled it from the pile and laid it over the opening.

It was just right, give or take an inch or two. Again, they were delivered from using the saw.

Now what they needed was something for fastening on the door. Charlie thought that he had some hinges in his culch pile that would work. He headed for the house while the other boys began to work on the walls of the clubhouse.

As Charlie reached the alley, something caught his eye by the trash cans at the far end of the block in back of Foley's house. It was a small upholstered chair. He hurried over to get a closer look.

It wasn't too bad. The wooden arms were scratched, and the back and seat, covered with a prickly green material, were a little worn and dirty, but there weren't any springs sticking out. He hadn't thought about furniture for the clubhouse, but this surely would make a good chair for just sitting and thinking out there in the clubhouse when they got it done. It really looked too good to throw away. He supposed he'd better ask, just to make sure it was all right to take it.

Charlie knocked at the Foley's back door.

Mrs. Foley answered the door, three sticky-faced little Foleys peering out from behind her.

"Oh, sure, Charlie," she said when Charlie had stated his business. "Take it along. We don't want it anymore."

"Thanks a lot!" Charlie said. Picking up the chair, he turned it upside down and carried it back up the alley on his head. The springs of the seat bounced and creaked comfortably above him, and the chair back thumped against his shoulder blades with every step.

In his excitement over his find, Charlie almost forgot why he had come to the house. Remembering just in time, he left the chair in the yard by the alley and went to get the hinges.

Back at the clubhouse with the hinges and the chair, Charlie was greeted with shouts of approval. The boys each took a turn trying out the chair and declared Charlie hero of the day.

Mike and Ben installed the hinges on the trap door, using some broad-headed nails. Charlie had a feeling that screws or bolts would have been better for fastening on hinges, but since he didn't have any screws that large, the nails would have to do.

The days rolled on toward the end of school. The clubhouse was coming along all right, considering everything. Something had to be done about windows and a roof, but it was going to be a very satisfactory clubhouse, Charlie was sure.

The trouble was, things were coming along in the garden, too.

"Weeds!" Aunt Essie exclaimed indignantly, coming in from looking at the garden early one morning before Ben and Charlie had left for school. "I'll give you boys a lesson in hoeing after school today." They glanced at each other. The clubhouse needed work, and Mike and Doug had already agreed to meet them, but there was nothing to be done about that. They would just have to tell them that the work was postponed.

The boys set off for school after Aunt Essie's announcement. It was the last week of school, ordinarily a time for celebration. But not this year.

"Vacation's going to be like going from the frying pan into the fire," Ben remarked gloomily.

"Yeah, some summer!" Charlie growled. He picked up a stone and skipped it down the street.

Chapter Eight
Hard Work

The garden grew unbelievably—and disgustingly—fast in the warm days of early summer. Ben and Charlie were kept busy with the thousand-and-one tasks that it took to keep everything up to Aunt Essie's standards of what a proper garden should be.

There was no doubt about it, Aunt Essie knew how to make a garden. She also knew how to keep two boys busy. What she didn't know was how to talk to two boys. And it must not have bothered her at all because she just went right on talking to herself in front of them as though they weren't there. Charlie was used to people like Pastor or Mrs. Watson at church or Dr. Blake the dentist, who would at least say "How are *you,* Charlie? Got any gadgets coming?" or "Building up your culch pile these days?"

Of course he knew that they weren't all *that* interested in his hobbies. It was just friendly interest, like waving at the mailman or saying "How are you today?" or talking about the weather. But Aunt Essie didn't care about being friendly. She was just interested in gardening. Moreover, her interest was not only in the vegetable garden, it extended to the whole yard. With the reluctant help of Ben and Charlie she had cleaned out the long-neglected borders that ran along both sides of the yard and the plantings around the house. Then there had been another excursion to Hatcher's for a wagonload of petunias and other flowering plants that Charlie couldn't remember the names of—not that he cared. He and Ben had to help plant them, too, while Red had stood on the border of the forbidden garden patch, trying to get them to pay attention to him.

Although their mother was pleased with the new look the yard was taking on, Ben and Charlie preferred the comfortable, rather unkempt, look of other years. They didn't mind mowing the lawn now and then when it got too long, but anything more was too much work and not worth the trouble. Worst of all, of course, with all the yard and garden work there wasn't enough time left to work on the clubhouse.

"It's not fair, the way Aunt Essie keeps thinking up stuff for us to do," Ben complained to their mother late one afternoon as she came into the yard from work. The boys still had to finish digging grass from the cracks in the front sidewalk.

"Yeah," Charlie said, "look what she's got us doing here. What's it matter if there's grass coming up between the cracks? If the grass wants to go to all that work to grow up between the cracks, we ought to let it."

"It looks a lot neater to me to have the grass cleaned out," Mom said. "Our little house is looking the best it has for years, thanks to you boys and Aunt Essie. I really appreciate all the work you've done."

"But we never have any time to work on the clubhouse, with all the work around here," Ben objected.

"You'd think we were slaves, with all the stuff she keeps thinking up for us to do," Charlie added.

"Well, now, I don't think it's that bad, is it, really?" she asked. "You do have time to work on your project. And the garden things will help out with our grocery spending. This could be a valuable experience for you both, if you'll go at it with the right attitude. Aunt Essie is an expert gardener, you know."

"I'm not going to have a garden when I grow up!" Ben said decidedly.

Charlie added his second to that. "Besides, she never even talks to us or says thank you when we help her. You always say thank you when we do our chores— even though we have to do them."

"Well, I admit that Aunt Essie is a little crusty, but she'll warm up to you, especially if you talk to her about gardening."

Charlie groaned. "I don't think she'll ever get to like us, and I don't think I could stand to hear anything else about gardens!"

"You never know!" their mother said cheerily. "In any case, *I* will say thank you for the wonderful job you've done on the garden and the lawn." And she gave Charlie a hug and opened her other arm to Ben. She smiled down at them. "You two might end up finding out that the Lord sent Aunt Essie to us for good reasons of His own—and not just the garden," she added, "but even if you never do, I'm glad that you've worked so hard for her. And the yard is beautiful." She gave them both another hug and then walked between them and up the steps into the house.

Even the Fourth of July was dominated by Aunt Essie. Ordinarily, Uncle Nate spent the holiday with the Scotts, and there would have been at least a trip to the state park for a day of swimming and picnicking, if not a longer excursion of some sort. This year, instead of a holiday with Uncle Nate, there was a Morgan family reunion at the village park in honor of Aunt Essie. Ben and Charlie had been to enough Morgan family reunions to know that this was not the choicest way to spend a Fourth of July. The reason was that there were no boys—or girls, either—Ben and Charlie's age. The Morgan family seemed to consist mainly of adults who, when they got together, sat around and ate and talked about old times.

The day more than exceeded the boys' expectations.

"The only good thing about today was the food," Ben said grumpily as the two crawled into bed that night, "but now my stomach doesn't feel good because I ate too much."

"Mine, either," Charlie said. "It feels like it's got a brick in it." Visions of fried chicken, baked ham, potato salad, macaroni salad, baked beans, cakes, and pies of all kinds floated unappealingly through Charlie's mind.

It had all tasted good at noon, and when it had been set out and passed around again late in the afternoon, it had still tasted good. Now, though, Charlie was sorry he had eaten so much.

"Wish we could have stayed home and worked on the clubhouse," Ben said, turning off the lamp on the table between the beds.

"I can't even remember what the clubhouse looks like," Charlie muttered. He rolled from his back to his stomach, and then to one side, trying to get comfortable.

"Probably won't even be able to find our way back there pretty soon, it'll be so grown up with weeds, if Aunt Essie doesn't quit thinking up stuff for us to do," Ben said with a yawn.

Charlie had a hard time getting to sleep that night because of the brick in his stomach. When he did sleep, he dreamed he was lost in a tangle of weeds that were taller than he was. And he couldn't find the clubhouse anywhere.

Chapter Nine
Senior Citizens to the Rescue

Surprisingly, there were no yard or garden chores the next morning, July the fifth. Aunt Essie herself said so! Ben and Charlie didn't ask questions. With Red riding comfortably in Charlie's side basket, they biked over to get Doug and Mike before she changed her mind.

Soon the gang was happily making its way to the Back Forty.

The clubhouse was still there in the same old place, contrary to Charlie's dream of the night before. And no weeds taller than Charlie had grown up in the path.

The tarpaulin that protected their building materials and other valuables sparkled with dew in the morning sunlight. Red barked at it and ran alongside, tail whipping back and forth as he waited for them to catch up. Ben and Mike pulled the tarpaulin off the pile and spread it on the bushes to dry.

"It looks to me like we're going to run out of boards before we finish the clubhouse," Doug said worriedly, looking at the pile of lumber.

Charlie had been thinking the same thing for quite a while, but he had been hoping that something would turn up, like another partition being torn out somewhere, or something. With all the yard and garden work, there hadn't been time for scouting around.

"What'll we do?" Mike asked. "We've still got the walls to finish."

"*And* the whole roof to put on," Doug added.

Strangely enough, there was something about need that put Charlie's brain in motion. Somehow he could find a way to achieve his purpose—like the time he had figured out how to get along without having to saw.

So now Charlie's brain went into gear.

The boys worked for a long while, pulling the sometimes rusty and bent nails out of the old boards and nailing them up one by one to make the walls.

"We're going to run out!" Doug worried every time they took a board off the diminishing pile.

Finally, after Doug had made his dire prediction for what seemed like the hundredth time, Charlie announced that he had an idea. His ideas had turned out to be pretty good lately, so the other boys were ready to listen.

"Okay," Charlie began. "We need windows, right?"

"Right."

"And we don't want to do any more sawing than we can help."

"Right again."

"So we make the walls just high enough to see over." Charlie stepped up on one of the porches. "This side is just high enough now," he decided. The other three walls were only one board shorter.

"What do we want to make the walls like that for?" Mike asked skeptically. "And what about windows?"

Charlie motioned to the empty space above the top board. "That could all be windows—all the way around above the tops of the walls to the roof."

"What about the roof?" Doug wanted to know.

"Yeah," Ben said, "even if we only use three more boards for the walls, we still don't have enough left for the whole roof."

"Just listen a minute, and I'll tell you," Charlie said a bit impatiently. "We can use what boards we have to make a sort of frame over the top and then—until we can find something better—we can use the tarp for a roof!"

"Hey, pretty good, Charlie!"

"That's using the old noggin!"

"Good deal!"

"We can finish the clubhouse—maybe today!"

The gang's voices rose, sounding pleased and excited.

Charlie felt rather pleased with his idea, too. "Okay, okay, a little less jaw work and a little more paw work," he interrupted, borrowing a saying he had picked up from one of the carpenters last summer.

They got busy with the paw work, and by the time the noon whistle blew, the walls were nearly finished.

Ben and Charlie hated to go in for lunch. Probably by this time Aunt Essie would have thought up something for them to do this afternoon. But they went anyway because they were hungry. Red, who knew what the noon whistle meant, rambled ahead of them.

"See you later," Doug and Mike called as they rode their bikes out of the yard.

"We hope!" Ben said.

Aunt Essie was nowhere in sight when the boys walked into the kitchen. Their mother, in her white uniform, was hurriedly setting things on the table. There was a pleasantly familiar array of peanut butter and jelly in jars, a loaf of bread in its wrapper, and a plastic refrigerator container of carrot and celery sticks. Just like old times. Before Aunt Essie.

"Man, that looks good!" Ben said appreciatively.

"Yeah, peanut butter and jelly sandwiches!" Charlie added, equally appreciative.

Their mother laughed. "I didn't know you were so fond of peanut butter and jelly sandwiches. Aunt Essie wanted to leave a casserole for us, but I told her we'd manage. She's gone on the senior citizen's tour, you know."

Ben and Charlie hadn't known, and they didn't care that she didn't leave a casserole. Hurray for the senior citizens! So that was why they'd had the whole morning to themselves. And now the whole afternoon? It was almost too much to take in!

The boys washed their hands and pitched in to help. Ben got the milk from the refrigerator, and Charlie gathered the silverware from the drawer, putting a knife at each place and a long-handled teaspoon like a flag in both of the jars.

They sat down at the table, and Mom asked the blessing. It seemed so good to sit down together, just the three of them again, that Charlie felt like saying amen aloud at the end of the prayer, but he didn't.

"When's Aunt Essie coming back?" Ben asked.

Charlie plastered a thick layer of peanut butter on a slice of bread, reached for the jelly, and wished his mother would answer, "Never!"

Instead, she said, "Oh, she'll be home this evening sometime."

This evening. Well, anyway, that gave them the whole afternoon to themselves again. And that brought Ben and Charlie's minds back to the clubhouse.

"We're gonna put the roof on the clubhouse this afternoon," Ben announced.

"Yeah," Charlie said. "Is it ever gonna be neat, Mom!"

"We were afraid we were going to run out of boards before we got the roof done," Ben told his mother, "but Charlie figured out a way to do it until we can find something better."

"Good for you, Charlie!" Mom said, smiling at Charlie. "Are you going to have open house or something when you've finished?"

The Back Forty had always been the boys' domain, and their mother rarely went back there without being invited.

"You could come back this afternoon when you get home from work," Ben said. "We'll have the roof on by that time."

And Aunt Essie won't be home, yet, to come along, Charlie thought. Somehow, he couldn't bear the idea of having Aunt Essie look at the clubhouse with her critical eye.

"All right, I'll do that," Mom said.

Chapter Ten
Up the Ladder
and Down Again

Finally the last boards for the walls of the clubhouse were nailed on.

"We'll need a ladder to do the roof," Doug said. "Haven't you guys got one in your garage?"

There was a ladder that had hung unused for years inside the garage. According to a discussion held long ago with their mother when Ben and Charlie were much younger, the ladder was supposed to stay hung up inside the garage.

Charlie looked at Ben, remembering. They had used the ladder one time to retrieve a toy glider from the garage roof. The ladder had slipped with both boys on it, and instead of getting the glider, they had each gotten a broken arm. That was when they had the discussion with their mother about leaving the ladder hung up inside the garage.

Uncle Nate had brought the glider down with a fishing pole while Ben and Charlie—each with an arm in a sling—watched and wished they had thought of using the fishing pole.

"What's the matter," Doug asked, looking from Ben to Charlie and then back to Ben again, "won't your mother let you use the ladder?"

"Well," Ben explained, smiling wryly, "the last time we used it we both got a broken arm, and Mom said we weren't to take it down again. But that was when we were little kids. I think she'd let us use it, but we'd better ask. I hope she's not too busy at Dr. Blake's. You come with me, Mike."

While Mike and Ben were gone, Doug and Charlie sorted through the remains of the lumber pile for boards long enough to make the roof. They found four that would do to nail around the tops of the two-by-fours above the windows for a framework. That left only three more boards long enough for the roof itself. Not enough, but that would have to do until something else turned up. It was good that they had the tarp.

Doug and Charlie sat down on one of the porches to pull out some nails from the roof boards. That finished, they impatiently waited for Ben and Mike to come back. Red, always curious over every change, nosed around the boards.

They came, finally, carrying the wooden ladder.

"She said we could use it," Ben announced. "Just be careful and all that stuff, you know. It was busy in Dr. Blake's office, and we had to wait a while to see her. That's what took so long."

The boys engineered the ladder into place at the corner of the clubhouse by the trap door. Ben stepped onto the bottom rung and bounced up and down to make sure it was firmly in place. Then while Doug held the ladder, Ben climbed up to work on the roof. Mike and Charlie handed up the first board. Red stayed in the background, eyeing the ladder distrustfully.

Taking turns with holding the ladder, handing up, and nailing, the boys put the few roof boards in place.

"Now then!" Mike announced in a fanfare sort of voice. "We put on the tarp, and we'll have a roof!"

They pulled the tarpaulin off the bushes where Ben and Mike had put it that morning and carried it to the ladder.

"Okay, here we go," Ben said, taking one corner of the canvas and scrambling up the ladder.

Suddenly, before anybody could do anything about it, Ben was in trouble. In his hurry, he tripped on the tarp. The ladder lurched. Ben gave a yelp as he began to fall.

Charlie didn't see what happened after that. The next thing he knew, he was seeing stars! Bright white ones flashing and whirling 'round and 'round. When the stars had gone away, he found himself lying on the ground, half covered with the tarp. Doug, Mike, and Ben leaned anxiously over him.

"You okay, Charlie?" they kept asking.

Charlie wasn't quite sure. Slowly he pushed off the tarp and pulled himself into a sitting position to get his bearings.

Some Summer!

As soon as he sat up, he knew he had a nosebleed. The blood gushed down his upper lip, into his mouth, and down his chin. He wiped it off with the back of his hand. And then he wished he hadn't.

"Somebody got a handkerchief or something?" Charlie asked desperately, feeling as though he were going to drown in his own blood.

Nobody had a handkerchief, but Mike generously donated a piece of his shirt.

"My mom won't care," he said as he ripped off a piece of shirttail. "She said earlier that this shirt was ready for the rag bag. Besides, it's an emergency."

Charlie sopped up the blood with the tail of Mike's shirt. "Thanks a lot!" he said.

"I can tear off another piece, if you need it," Mike offered.

"You'd better start tearing," Charlie said. "This'll be used up in a minute."

"Lie down, Charlie," Ben advised. "That'll help stop a nosebleed."

Charlie lay down. The blood ran more slowly from his nose, but now he could feel it running down inside his throat. Yuk! His nose was beginning to hurt a little, now, too.

Charlie sat up. He preferred the blood running down the outside rather than the inside. Finally, he struggled to his feet, holding the improvised handkerchief to his nose. He had to have a drink to get rid of that awful salty blood taste, and maybe something cold to put on his nose.

"I'm going to the house to get a drink of water," he announced through the wad of Mike's blood-soaked shirttail.

"We'll come with you," Ben said.

By the time they got to the house, the second shirttail handkerchief was thoroughly saturated.

"You're dripping blood all over," Doug said worriedly as they headed for the bathroom. "Our mom would kill us!"

"Aw, it'll clean up," Ben assured him.

Depositing the soaked rag in the wastebasket, Charlie turned on the cold water faucet and splashed water onto his face to wash away the blood. He slurped up some water from his hands, ran it around in his mouth, spit it out, then slurped and spit some more. Still the blood gushed from his nose.

"You've got to lie down," Ben said insistently, "or you'll never get it stopped. Do you want to bleed to death?"

Charlie thought not. He lay down on the mat beside the bathtub. Red, unused to such proceedings, paced up and down alongside him.

"Man!" Doug exclaimed, "now you're bleeding all over the rug." He pulled off a long length of toilet tissue, wadded it up and handed it to Charlie.

"What you need is something cold to stop the bleeding," Ben remembered now. "I'll be right back."

He returned shortly with one of the frozen cloths their mother kept in the freezer for such emergencies.

Ben lay the stiff, cold cloth on Charlie's nose.

"Ouch! That hurts!" Charlie objected and started to take the cloth off his tender nose.

"No, wait," Ben said firmly. "It'll soften up in a minute."

Charlie waited, enduring the cloth and the unpleasantness of blood running down his throat. Gradually the cloth softened and the cold began to make his nose feel better. When the cloth was completely thawed and no longer cold, Ben brought another from the freezer, rinsed out the first one and put it back to get cold.

Finally, after several applications with the frozen cloths, the bleeding stopped. Charlie, feeling rather groggy, but glad that his nose wasn't dripping anymore, got to his feet.

While they had been waiting for the bleeding to stop, the other boys had wiped up the blood Charlie had dripped across the floor. Except for the bath mat—they didn't know what to do about that—the floor was as clean as before.

"I don't know about you guys," Ben said, "but I'm hungry." He went into the kitchen, the rest of the gang following.

The cookie jar was half full of Aunt Essie's big, round, sugar-raisin cookies. Sitting around the table, the boys devoured these with some milk, and Charlie began to feel like himself again.

"What happened, anyway?" Charlie asked as they ate. "What did I hit my nose on? All I remember is Ben tripping on the tarp."

"I fell off the ladder and hit you on the way down," Ben said, "but it didn't hurt me."

"And he knocked you into those floor boards that stick out," Mike told Charlie.

"I sure am sorry," Ben apologized. "I was in too big a hurry."

"That's all right. I was in a hurry, too, to get the roof on the clubhouse." Charlie paused to swallow the last of his milk and to wipe his mouth on the back of his hand, then added, "I'm still in a hurry. Let's get going!"

Back at the clubhouse they again turned to the task of putting on the roof. This time Ben went more slowly up the ladder, the other boys handing the tarp up to him as he went, and keeping it to one side so he wouldn't trip on it again. Red liked the ladder even less this time, and barked a warning every now and then.

It was more than just one boy could do to get the tarp spread out over the top of the clubhouse. This was where the porches again came in handy. By standing on the overhang and using some short pieces of boards like arms, they pulled the tarp across. When they finally got it in place, they discovered that it was so large that it hung down over the windows, which was a good thing. That way, the hole in the corner of the tarp didn't matter.

Charlie pointed out another advantage. "We can fold it back out of the way when the weather's nice, and when it's not, we can let it hang down to keep out the cold and rain," he said.

So they nailed it to the roof boards to hold it in place. Then, the day being sunny, they folded two sides of the tarp up onto the roof.

"Man, that's neat!" Mike exclaimed as they all stepped back to admire their work. "Let's see how it is inside."

Charlie was nearest the trap door. He scooted under the clubhouse, pushed up the door and crawled in. As the other boys were making their way through the trap door, Charlie stood there feeling cosily enclosed by the walls and roof of the clubhouse. A thrill of achievement ran through him, even though the roof wasn't all he might have wished. He thought he must know a little of the way God had felt when He had finished creating the world.

"Man, we built us a clubhouse!" Ben said after a few moments of admiring silence.

"Yeah!" the others said in an awed tone.

Chapter Eleven
Celebration

"Ben? Charlie?" their mother called from outside.

Charlie couldn't believe it was time for her to come home from work already. He had never known an afternoon to go so fast in all his life. Red scooted outside the door to welcome her.

"We're in here, Mom," Ben called.

"Who's hurt?" she asked in a worried voice.

"Uh-oh!" Doug said under his breath.

"We're okay, Mom," Ben assured her, making his way through the trap door. "We just had a little accident, and Charlie got a bloody nose."

"From the looks of the bath mat and the bathroom sink, I was afraid there'd been a massacre," their mom said.

Charlie, followed by Mike and Doug, emerged from under the clubhouse.

His mother looked at him with a shocked expression. "Charlie! Are you sure there hasn't been a massacre?"

Charlie looked down at his blood-spattered T-shirt and jeans and realized for the first time that he was quite a startling sight. He shrugged. "It was just a really bloody nosebleed," he said.

"That must be the understatement of the year," their mom said. She looked closely at Charlie's nose. "I think your nose is a little swollen. Does it hurt?"

"No, not much."

"Whatever happened?" she wanted to know.

The boys went over the details until she was satisfied that the accident wasn't really serious.

"You boys and that ladder," she said, shaking her head.

"Mom, how do you like our clubhouse?" Ben asked.

Charlie was glad that Ben was getting their mother's thoughts away from the ladder. If she got to thinking about it too much, she might again decide that they couldn't use it. And then how could they finish the roof—when they found some materials?

Ben and Charlie's mother followed as the boys took her on a tour around the outside of the clubhouse.

Ben pointed out the porches that had saved a lot of sawing and would come in handy for all kinds of uses. Doug stepped up on one and demonstrated the convertibility of the temporary tarpaulin roof.

"Want to see the inside, Mrs. Scott?" Mike asked.

She laughed. "I was just wondering how you get inside. I've seen all four sides of your clubhouse—I think—but I haven't seen a door. Did you forget to put one in?"

While she was talking, Charlie scooted under the clubhouse and through the trap door. "Hi, Mom," he said, peering over the walls of the clubhouse at the four standing outside.

"Charlie, how did you get in there?" his mother asked.

"We've got a trap door! Show her, you guys."

Ben, Mike, and Doug crawled under the clubhouse and joined Charlie on the inside.

"Come on in," they invited.

She looked down at her white uniform. "I think I'd better wait until I'm dressed more suitably for crawling through trap doors. Thanks, anyway. You've built quite a clubhouse. We ought to have a celebration of some sort. How about a hamburger fry in the back yard tonight for the four of you?"

They all thought that sounded like a good idea and said so loudly.

Mom went to the house to make arrangements with Doug and Mike's mother for the boys to stay, and to get things started for supper.

With Red getting in the way every now and then, the boys put the best of the remaining building materials and the green upholstered chair inside the clubhouse in case it should rain. The trap door, they discovered, was not the handiest way to take things inside. They had quite a struggle with the chair, in particular. Finally, they hoisted it over the top of the wall.

By the time they got to the house, there was a charcoal fire going, and Mom was spreading a red, white, and blue checked cloth on the picnic table in the back yard.

"Charlie," she said, looking up as the boys came across the lawn, "I think we'd all enjoy our supper more if you took a bath and put on clean clothes."

The idea of taking a bath right now didn't appeal to Charlie at all, but he supposed his bloody clothes didn't look very appetizing. Reluctantly he went to clean up while the others helped with the supper.

The hamburger fry turned out to be a real celebration. The hamburgers were thick, brown, and juicy with a slice of cheese melted over them and mustard, ketchup, and pickle relish. There was chocolate milk for a special treat. And, for an extra-special treat, watermelon. Charlie had seen a truckload of them go by just after lunch, but it had seemed too much to hope that his mother would buy one.

All this, and no Aunt Essie. It seemed like a hundred years since Charlie had enjoyed such a good and satisfying day.

After supper the clubhouse, like a magnet, drew the boys to the Back Forty. They hung around admiring their handiwork and planning what to do next until almost dark, when the mosquitoes—out in full force— drove them back to the house.

The coals on the grill were still hot—just right for roasting marshmallows. So the boys roasted marsh- mallows and slapped mosquitoes. There weren't so many of the pesky insects near the house as there had been out in the Back Forty, but there were enough to be a nuisance.

Fireflies, like tiny flashing neon lights, flitted about in the twilight. It would be nice, Charlie thought, if mosquitoes came equipped with lights, too. Then you could see them and catch them before they bit.

Chapter Twelve
Dry Weather

A hot, dry spell came in the first part of July. The neighbors' gardens were drooping from lack of water, but not Aunt Essie's. She saw to it that the plants got the necessary moisture to keep them thriving and healthy. This, of course, was Ben and Charlie's job.

It would have been a simple task, and maybe even fun, had they been able to use the garden hose. However, the hose wasn't long enough to reach as far as the garden. The boys had to haul water with the faithful old wagon.

"I thought a wagon was to have fun with. All we ever do with it is work!" Charlie grumbled one scorching July morning.

Ben's prediction about going from the frying pan into the fire had come true in more ways than one. It was so hot that at first the water ran warm out of the hose when he turned it on.

Charlie held the hose to fill the old washtub that they had set in the wagon to carry water. It felt good when the warm water had drained out of the hose and began to run cold. He flopped the end of the hose up and down, allowing the water to splash out on himself and Ben, leaving cool wet spots on their T-shirts and jeans.

Red, who had been lying in the shade of the shrubbery by the garage, ambled over, tail wagging, to see what was going on.

When the tub was full, Charlie put his thumb over the end of the hose and squirted himself and Ben until there were more cool wet spots on their clothing than dry ones. Then, since Red seemed to be expecting something, Charlie gave him a good spraying.

They were just beginning to have fun when Aunt Essie appeared at the kitchen window scowling and shaking her head disapprovingly.

Reluctantly Ben went to turn off the water.

Red shook himself violently, sending a shower of water in all directions as if to express his feelings—and Ben and Charlie's—toward the interference. That for meddling aunts!

The boys grumbled as they sloshed out to water the garden. Why couldn't Aunt Essie mind her own business? It was bad enough that she made them work. Did she have to spoil their fun, too? Why hadn't she stayed in Florida where she belonged? Just when their mother had decided they didn't need a sitter anymore, Aunt Essie had to show up. It wasn't fair!

The more they thought about it, the angrier they became. And the angrier they became, the more frustrated they felt because there wasn't a thing they

could do about the situation except get angry. Aunt Essie was here for the summer, and that was that. There was no getting around Aunt Essie.

Ben and Charlie finished their chores by noon and went sullenly into the house for lunch.

Aunt Essie always saw to it that the family sat down to a proper meal. And as usual, she ruined it by ruling the conversation with their mother, while the boys sat in ignored silence. There was no arguing the fact that she was a good cook. Sometimes she even fixed something special for dessert. Be that as it may, had she served fried chicken and banana cream pie today—which she hadn't (there was macaroni and cheese and canned peaches)—Charlie would have preferred a peanut butter sandwich he'd made himself. Aunt Essie could take her proper meals back to Florida, fried chicken and all!

Nobody was in a very good mood when the gang got together that afternoon. Even Doug and Mike were edgy.

They trudged along what was now a well-worn path across the Back Forty to the clubhouse. Although the trees here were not large, there were enough of them, and they were close enough together to make some shade. A slight breeze stirred, helping to give at least an illusion of coolness.

On the shady side of the clubhouse, the boys lolled on the grass under the trees, slurping water and crunching ice cubes that Doug and Mike had brought along from home. Nobody said anything for a while.

Suddenly Doug interrupted the ice cube crunching. "It's crooked," he stated decidedly, as though someone else had made a wrong statement that needed correcting.

"Huh?" Ben, Mike, and Charlie mumbled together indifferently. If something was crooked, it would have to stay that way. It was too hot to even care.

"The clubhouse," Doug insisted, "look at it. Doesn't it look crooked to you guys?"

Charlie, Ben, and Mike roused themselves enough to look at the clubhouse.

With a sinking feeling, Charlie saw that Doug was right. There was a very definite tilt toward the south.

"Aw," Ben said, "it just tilts a little. That doesn't hurt anything."

"No, not yet, but what if it gets worse?" Doug wanted to know.

Charlie thought of the famous leaning tower in Italy that he had seen in a travel film at school last year. He remembered it particularly because in one of the pictures a man had posed beside it in such a way that it looked as though he were pushing it over. What was the name of that building? Oh yes, he remembered.

"It'll be the Leaning Tower of Pizza!" Charlie said aloud and then wished immediately that he hadn't.

The other three boys laughed and guffawed loudly. "Pizza! The Leaning Tower of Pizza!"

"Not *Pizza*," Doug said in an annoyingly superior tone, "Pisa."

In his already dark mood from the events of the morning and the miserably hot day, Charlie felt like socking the three of them—and especially Doug—in the nose. Pizza . . . Pisa. It wasn't that funny, but he'd probably never hear the last of it.

Charlie got up, went over to the clubhouse and crawled underneath, hoping the three laughing hyenas wouldn't follow him. As he pushed up on the trap door, one of the hinges pulled loose. That was just what he had thought would happen. Nails were not for holding hinges. They needed screws.

He crawled through the opening, put the door back in its place and sat on it, as if to barricade himself from the rest of the irritating world.

It was miserably hot inside the clubhouse, but it felt almost good to be miserably hot. Nothing was going right. Charlie could feel the slant of the floor as he sat on the trap door. Absently he took a marble out of his pocket and rolled it toward the opposite wall along the ridge where the extra boards were nailed on to make an opening for the trap door. The marble rolled quickly back to him. Had he been in a better mood, it might have been an interesting game.

The laughter outside had stopped. Charlie heard Mike ask in a hushed voice, "Is he mad?"

"Oh, he doesn't stay mad long," Ben said.

It seemed to Charlie as though he had been angry for a long, long time. Not at Ben and Mike and Doug really, though they needn't have made such a fuss about his mistake, but at Aunt Essie for messing up the whole summer. Had he been that angry at the other boys, he would have really socked them, and they could have had a good fight and been done with it. Being angry at Aunt Essie, though—well, that was something different. It was like having a wild animal caged inside him wanting to get out to snap and snarl and bite. But it couldn't. It had to stay quietly in its cage.

After a while there was a scuffling under the clubhouse, and Charlie felt someone pushing on the trap door.

"Charlie? You mad at us?" Mike called.

"I don't like being laughed at," Charlie said.

"We're sorry," Doug said. "What you said just struck us funny."

"Well, it wasn't that funny!"

There was another push on the trap door.

"Hey, Charlie, let us in," Ben said.

Charlie slid off the door and lifted it up so that the others wouldn't notice that the hinge was loose. He wanted to point out this flaw himself.

Ben, Doug, and Mike crawled in and Charlie replaced the door.

"Man, it's hot in here!" Mike exclaimed, hanging his tongue out to pant like a dog and fanning himself with his hand.

"Hey," Doug said, "You can even tell the clubhouse slants from in here."

"Yeah, I know," Charlie said dejectedly. "Look." He rolled the marble across the floor. They watched silently and slightly stupefied from the heat as Charlie rolled the marble back and forth.

"Sure does slant," Mike observed unnecessarily, panting and fanning himself again.

"Must be for some reason the stilts on that side have sunk deeper into the ground," Charlie said, feeling as though nothing about the clubhouse or even life itself could ever be good again.

"What's to stop 'em from sinking more?" Doug asked.

"Nothing," Charlie said gloomily, still rolling the marble back and forth.

"Let's go out and take a look," Ben said.

"Yeah," Mike said, "if we stay in here, there'll be nothing left of us but four pools of melted—"

"Oops!" Ben interrupted as he lifted the trap door. "One of the hinges is coming off!"

"Yeah," Charlie said, not really caring, after all, that the hinge problem had been discovered. He gave the marble one last roll, picked it up and put it in his pocket. "We need some screws for the hinges."

"We ought to be able to scrape up enough money between the four of us to buy some screws," Doug said.

"Let's go down to the hardware store and see how much screws that big would cost," Ben suggested. He wiped his sweaty face with the back of his hand. "It's air-conditioned down there, remember? Come on!"

Charlie watched as Mike, Ben, and Doug disappeared through the trap-door opening. He almost felt like staying here and being miserable all by himself in the heat. However, a small light had begun to shine at the top of Charlie's pit of gloom. At least they could fix the hinges. And it was always the most fun to go into

Folsom's Hardware when you really wanted to buy something.

Charlie scrambled through the opening in the floor and hurried to catch up with the others.

It took two trips to town to get the screws. They couldn't be sure what size they needed because nobody had thought to measure or to bring the hinge along. So they had to go back to the clubhouse. Since Charlie couldn't find his six-foot-two-inch ruler at the moment, they wrenched the hinge from the one remaining nail that was holding it to the floor of the clubhouse and took it along.

To Charlie's disappointment, Mr. Folsom wasn't in the store this afternoon. There were just the two lady clerks. Mr. Folsom was friendly and always had time to talk and answer questions. He didn't care how long anybody took looking around. The lady clerks—Charlie didn't know their names—hovered nervously over the boys, watching their every move.

"They make me feel like they think I'm going to steal something," Mike whispered.

Ben and Charlie had complained to their mother not long ago about the hovering clerks.

"They don't know you as Mr. Folsom does," she had explained, "and the storekeepers do have trouble with a few of the children around town stealing things."

It was hard to understand how anybody could take something that didn't belong to him, but Charlie remembered very dimly when he had done that very thing once. It was such a long time ago that it seemed as though it were somebody else who had done it. He had taken a little toy car from Mr. Benson's drug store. His mother had discovered it before they got home. She had made him take it back to Mr. Benson, and Charlie had learned that he wasn't to take something from the store without paying for it. And that was good, he thought.

The four boys were heading toward home, having finally bought twelve good, sturdy-looking screws, when Doug came to a sudden halt in front of the barber shop.

"Oh, no!" he said, pointing to a poster in the window. "I thought maybe they'd forgotten about that this summer for once."

"Daily Vacation Bible School," Ben read the poster aloud. "Learning to Know God . . . MacArthur Community Church . . . July 19-23 . . . 9:30-11:30 A.M."

"Oh, they've been talking about that in Sunday school for ages," Mike said.

"Do you think they ever will forget?" Ben asked. "Not while Mrs. Watson breathes!"

Mrs. Watson was the very determined lady who had directed Vacation Bible School ever since Charlie could remember. For some mysterious reason, which probably had something to do with Mrs. Watson, practically every boy and girl in MacArthur from three years old on up to ninth grade went to Bible school, regardless of whether he attended church the rest of the year. Even Butch Kelley, who was the toughest kid in town that Charlie could think of, went to Bible school. If they couldn't get there any other way, Mrs. Watson went and got them in her red van. Charlie even remembered seeing Mrs. Watson carry Stevie Hawks back and forth from the van to the church the year Stevie had both legs in a cast because of a car accident.

"Good ol' Mrs. Watson," Mike mused. "She's kinda nice, though, somehow or other."

Charlie had to agree, though he couldn't understand it. Mrs. Watson was a little pushy, but you couldn't help liking her. There were worse things than going to Bible school. Like working in Aunt Essie's garden. It was just that nobody relished the idea of anything with the name of school attached to it right in the middle of summer vacation.

Anyway, there was the inescapable fact. Bible school, July 19-23. And July 19 was next Monday. The gang resigned itself to the prospect as it installed the screws in the hinges for the trap door.

Chapter Thirteen
Vacation Bible School

A brief, warm shower came on Monday morning, but it wasn't the rain everybody had been hoping for to cool things off. At the church Ben, Mike, and Charlie filed into the corner basement room with the rest of the fifth and sixth graders of the community. Doug was with the junior high group upstairs.

The basement had felt fairly cool as they came down the stairs. By the time everybody had found a seat and the door was closed, the coolness had gone. The atmosphere was steamy and smelled like a soggy dog. Probably it was everybody's wet socks and sneakers, Charlie thought.

From his back row seat Charlie looked over this year's teacher, a man by the name of Lee Hopkins, who was a good friend of Uncle Nate. He was a tall man with steel gray hair, older than Uncle Nate, but not really old. He had a farm on the road between MacArthur and Hamilton. Ben and Charlie had been there with Uncle Nate.

Mr. Hopkins was saying something about learning Bible verses when Charlie tuned in to what was going on in class.

Marty Thomas, on the front row, waved his hand and, without waiting to be recognized, asked eagerly, "What do we get if we learn all the verses?"

The whole class shifted uncomfortably. Marty was the one who always won the prizes when it came to learning verses.

Mr. Hopkins smiled a little and said he didn't figure it was fitting to pay anybody to learn Bible verses. "Would I have to pay you to get you to take a flashlight to find your way in the dark?" he asked. Then he explained that the teachings of the Bible were like a light to help people find their way safely through life.

That matter settled, Mr. Hopkins began the lesson by asking a question that unsettled Charlie.

"How do you know that God is real?"

It was not that Mr. Hopkins had any idea that He wasn't. The question was, *how* do *you* know?

The class was perfectly silent for a long moment. Had Mr. Hopkins handed out lesson books, somebody would have been shuffling through the pages looking for the answer, but Mr. Hopkins hadn't handed out any lesson books. Charlie had a feeling that the answer to that question wasn't to be found in a lesson book, anyway.

Finally, John Stewart raised his hand. "I know God is real," he said slowly, "because when I get up in the morning and start out to have a bad day and then I pray about it, it turns out to be a good day."

Charlie looked at John sitting in the row ahead of him. Smiling, friendly John with whom Charlie had gone to school ever since kindergarten. It was hard to imagine John ever having a bad day. Well, maybe he didn't. He prayed about it before it ever got to the whole day.

Charlie was a little surprised to see Ben raise his hand. "I know God is real because Jesus saved me, and Jesus is the Son of God. He rose from the dead."

"Good," Mr. Hopkins commented, but still he didn't jump right in with a list of ways that everybody could know that God was real. Instead, he let the class discuss the question, putting in a few words himself now and then. He seemed not to be bothered at all by long silences, stupid questions, or even wrong answers. All in all, it was an interesting session. Even so, by dismissal time, Charlie still hadn't found a satisfactory answer to the question for himself.

Mr. Hopkins told them to read the the first chapter of John to find out what it said about God. Charlie didn't like having homework, but he decided to do it.

At noon the sun was shining again, hot as ever. Except for settling the dust a little, it might just as well not have rained at all. There were green beans to be picked, and Ben and Charlie had been hoping for an all-day rain. No such luck.

Charlie thought about Mr. Hopkins' question as he, Ben, and Aunt Essie picked beans. Aunt Essie's presence turned off anything in the way of an interesting

conversation, so there was nothing to do but think—
and pick beans.

How do I know God is real? Charlie asked himself.
He couldn't remember ever thinking that He wasn't. Both
at home and at church he had been taught about God
from the Bible. He believed that what he had been taught
was true, which was a good beginning, he supposed,
but now there seemed to be more to it than that. How
do *I* know God is real? Charlie asked himself again.
Not just because somebody says He is, but how do *I*
know?

He still hadn't come up with an answer by the time
the beans were picked, except that he thought maybe
next time he started to have a bad day he'd try John
Stewart's solution. He'd pray about it and see what
happened.

Charlie's next bad day actually started that evening.
After supper he and Ben were out on the front steps
trying to keep cool when Doug and Mike appeared.
What irritated Charlie was that he and Ben had been
having their own conversation about God, and it wasn't
a good time to be interrupted. Ben had already read
John 1. "It's the part about Jesus being the Word," Ben
told him. "And being there from the beginning with God
and then becoming a man."

"John knew all that because he talked to Jesus and
saw Him do miracles," Charlie said.

Just then Doug and Mike rode into the yard on
their bikes.

"Hey, you guys," Doug yelled, "let's go out to the Pizza House!" He roared with laughter.

At first nobody caught on. There was a Pizza House Restaurant in Hamilton. Uncle Nate sometimes took the Scotts there for Friday night supper. Not since Aunt Essie had come, though. She didn't care for pizza.

"Don't you get it?" Doug prodded. "Leaning Tower of Pizza House!"

Then Ben and Mike laughed, too.

Charlie didn't laugh. He didn't think much of the joke. He didn't think much of Doug, either, for remembering his mistake. Doug always thought he was smart because he was the oldest. Somebody ought to take him down a notch or two, Charlie thought grimly.

The other boys didn't seem to notice that Charlie was not enjoying the joke.

"Okay," Ben said, getting up. "Let's go to the Pizza House. Can't be any hotter back there than it is here. Come on, Red."

Charlie stayed on the step, feeling as though a thunderstorm were brewing inside him.

"Aren't you coming, Charlie?" Mike asked.

"Naw, it's too hot," he said, keeping the thunderstorm mostly to himself.

The other boys, followed by Red, disappeared around the corner of the house without him. Charlie didn't care. He didn't want to hear any more about Doug's stupid Pizza House.

Charlie had a hard time getting to sleep that night. It was hot, for one thing, but that wasn't his biggest problem. He tossed and turned trying to think of some way to get back at Doug for making fun of his Leaning Tower of Pizza mistake. The trouble was, Doug didn't seem to realize that it made Charlie angry. On top of that, Charlie had to admit that it really was kind of a silly thing to be angry about.

Charlie pictured himself giving Doug a good sock in the nose. "There," he would say, "that's for laughing because I said pizza instead of Pisa."

Just the thought of admitting that he was still angry about that made Charlie feel as embarrassed as he was angry. He sat up, shook out his crumpled, sweaty pillow and gave it a poke. Then he lay down to toss and turn some more.

When Charlie woke the next morning, he felt as though he had not slept at all. Ben, already out of bed, was looking out the window that faced the back yard.

"I wonder if she ever sleeps," Ben mumbled sleepily.

The "she" Ben was talking about, no doubt, was Aunt Essie. Charlie had wondered the same thing himself.

He pried himself out of bed and went to look out the window with Ben. He still felt weighted down by his anger of last night. He couldn't talk about it with Ben, though. He'd think it was silly, too. However, Charlie could easily transfer that anger to Aunt Essie. That he could talk about with Ben.

Aunt Essie, he saw, was in the garden, a basket on her arm, gathering leaf lettuce.

"She's always up and doing things when we get up, and she's still up and doing things when we go to bed," Ben continued.

"And thinking up stuff for us to do," Charlie added, his teeth clenched.

"I'll bet that's what she's doing right now," Ben said. "It makes me so mad I could . . . I could . . . spit!"

"Me, too! Why did she have to come along and spoil our whole summer?"

Both boys glared through the window at Aunt Essie.

With the outside angry feeling toward Aunt Essie, and the inside angry feeling toward Doug left over from last night, the day was definitely off to a bad start. Way in the back of his mind, Charlie knew that this was exactly the sort of day that John Stewart would pray about. But Charlie was in no mood to pray.

Chapter Fourteen
A Camp Out

Charlie's bad day that began on Monday night stretched all the way to Friday. While his anger toward Doug for the Leaning Tower of Pizza joke slowly faded, his feelings toward Aunt Essie, whose offenses increased both in quantity and quality as the days passed, were something else again.

Just when the boys were going to hunt lumber scraps, she would tell them to hoe or pick lettuce or water the garden. And whenever Ben and Charlie were talking about something while they worked—even John 1, which they were studying for Vacation Bible School—Aunt Essie would show up and start talking in that annoying way to herself. It was always comments like, "Well, the tomatoes are ripening," or "Bugs haven't taken over yet." Nothing that needed an answer, but enough to prevent Ben and Charlie from having their own conversation.

Between everything that she thought up for Ben and Charlie to do, and having to go to Bible school every morning, there was little time left for solving problems back at the clubhouse. Besides that, the sessions at Bible school had left Charlie squirmy and restless with more questions than he had answers.

Doug, Mike, Ben, and Charlie crossed the church parking lot toward home Friday noon, Bible school over for another year. The sun beat down hot and close. It was so hot Charlie thought he could almost break the heat off in pieces.

The heat must have been good for hatching ideas, though, for suddenly one hatched that promised to bring the week to a better ending than its beginning. Afterward, nobody could have said who hatched the idea, but there it was.

Camp out . . . tonight . . . at the clubhouse!

"I just hope Mom will let us," Charlie said. "She's kind of funny about letting us do stuff after dark, you know."

"Well, we can hope," Ben said.

Doug and Mike felt sure that if Ben and Charlie's mother gave her permission, their parents would, too.

The gang, along with Red, descended upon her as she came into the yard for her noon break. Ben brought up the big question.

She looked skeptical. "It's a long way back there in the dark all by yourselves," she objected.

"Not any farther than it is in the daylight, Mom," Ben reminded her.

"No, I suppose not," she said slowly as though she wasn't really sure about that.

"We'll take Red," Charlie said. "He's a good watch dog."

Their mother looked doubtfully at Red, his ardently wagging tail pleading the cause.

Fortunately the conversation was interrupted by the familiar two short honks of a car horn as Uncle Nate's blue station wagon rolled in the driveway. It wasn't often that he came this early, but he couldn't have come at a better time, Charlie thought.

After the usual greetings, Mom asked Uncle Nate what he thought about the boys' idea.

"Oh, sure! They'll be okay," he assured her. "Tom Potter and I used to camp out all the time when we were their age, remember? Only we didn't have a clubhouse to sleep in. We slept out on the ground."

Good old Uncle Nate! The boys looked at one another triumphantly. Mom could certainly see that he had survived under even more perilous circumstances than what they had in mind.

At last she gave her permission for the camp out.

There were more green beans to pick that afternoon.

Uncle Nate helped with that task; then he, Ben, and Charlie snipped the ends off the beans while Aunt Essie cut them up and put them in containers for the freezer.

Somehow when Uncle Nate was around, Aunt Essie didn't keep up her patter of talking to herself.

"What'd you learn in Vacation Bible School this week?" he asked as they worked at the kitchen table.

"John 1," both boys said.

Charlie wanted to add that he hadn't learned very much—all he had gotten was a lot of questions. But he didn't want to say that in front of Aunt Essie, so instead he asked, "How do *you* know, for yourself, that God is real, Uncle Nate?"

"Well, the Bible for one thing," Uncle Nate told him. "Its words have a way of piercing through things." He tossed a handful of beans into a bowl on the table. "For another thing, I believe that the resurrection of Jesus has been proved beyond doubt. But I guess the biggest thing is that—being saved—I have the Holy Spirit in me that witnesses those things to me."

Charlie didn't say anything. He had gotten saved two years ago. At first he had felt like God was always right near him, but pretty soon it had begun to seem like life had gone back to normal.

Uncle Nate seemed to read his thoughts. "A person has to give heed to the Spirit, of course, by reading Scripture and praying and meditating on what God says," he added.

When the beans were finally taken care of, Ben and Charlie went to collect what they needed for the camp out.

"Wish we had some sleeping bags," Charlie said as they rummaged in the cedar chest in the upstairs hall for something to sleep on.

"At least we don't need anything for keeping warm," Ben said.

They found some old quilts that would do, and, rolling them up with their pillows in the middle, tied them with twine that Charlie had stuck away in his dresser drawer.

"Now something for supper," Ben said as they thumped down the stairs with their bed rolls. They had planned before Mike and Doug left at noon that their supper would be a sort of potluck with each of them bringing whatever they could find handy at home that wouldn't take dishes or cooking.

The aroma of liver and onions that Aunt Essie was cooking for supper permeated the house. Liver and onions smelled good, Charlie thought, because of the onions. When it came to eating them, he always wished it was something other than liver with the onions. He didn't feel as though he were missing anything by not eating at home this evening. Besides, there'd be green beans, and he was tired of looking at green beans, to say nothing of eating them.

Happily, Aunt Essie was out of the kitchen at the moment, so they were free to make up their supper menu without any interference. Quickly, Charlie took a grocery bag from the drawer by the kitchen sink and he and Ben raided the refrigerator and cupboards.

Mom came home from work as the boys set their camping supplies outside the back door. She peeked into the grocery bag, smiled, and shook her head.

"You don't want to stay and have liver and onions with us?" she teased.

"Nope!" Ben and Charlie said together.

"Have you got a flashlight?" she asked.

"I think Mike and Doug are bringing one," Ben said.

At that moment the Grandy brothers glided into the yard on their bikes and came to a screeching halt by the back door.

"Did you guys bring a flashlight?" Ben asked.

For answer, Doug pulled a flashlight from his back pocket and turned it on.

"Good," Mom said, nodding approval. "Now, no building a fire. You know that," she added very firmly.

"No, we won't," all four boys assured her. They had been over all that at noon. As dry as it was, the whole town of MacArthur would be gone in nothing flat if a fire ever got out of control. Besides, who needed a fire, as hot as it was, anyway?

"Well, if the mosquitoes get bad or anything, you can come back up to the house, you know," Mom said hopefully.

"We will, Mom," Ben said.

The boys loaded their gear on their bikes and set off across the back yard followed by Red.

"Have fun," Uncle Nate called from the back door, and Aunt Essie even waved from the kitchen window. Back at the clubhouse, the boys stuffed their sleeping gear through the trap door.

"Whew!" Mike said as they crawled out from under the clubhouse. "It sure is hot in there! Hope it cools down by the time we want to go to bed."

"Probably won't get very cool," Doug said.

"Man," Charlie said, "it's been hot so long, I don't think I even remember what cool feels like."

"Well, hot or not, let's eat. After a hard afternoon in the bean patch, I'm hungry," Ben declared.

They set the food out on the porch on the shadiest side of the clubhouse.

"That makes a neat table," Doug said. "Sometimes you get some pretty good ideas, Charlie."

"Thanks!" Charlie said with a grin. He felt quite forgiving now toward Doug.

"Looks like we've got ourselves a pretty good supper," Mike said, looking over the array of food.

There were two parts of loaves of bread, one whole wheat that Ben and Charlie had brought, and a half-loaf of raisin bread that Mike and Doug had brought. There were two jars of peanut butter, both crunchy, one from each house. Mike and Doug had also brought half a package of sliced bologna, some vanilla wafers, and a large package of potato chips. Then there was a jar of cheese spread from the Scotts and some of Aunt Essie's chocolate chip cookies.

They hadn't brought anything to drink except a plastic jug of water that Ben had thought of at the last minute.

"Hey, we didn't bring any cups!" Doug exclaimed.

"Aw, we can all drink out of the jug," Ben said. "What's a few germs among friends?"

"Maybe I won't get thirsty," Doug said.

"Uh-oh! We forgot knives, too," Ben said.

"We've got jackknives, haven't we?" Charlie reminded him.

"Oh, yeah, good," Ben said. "I was afraid we'd have to go back and get some. Can't spread peanut butter very well with your fingers."

Charlie pulled his knife from his pocket and opened it, not letting himself try to remember what he'd used it for last in case it had been something like scraping mud from his sneakers. He guessed it couldn't have been that, though, since it had been a long time since there'd been any mud.

Wiping the blade of his knife on his T-shirt, he looked over the food.

"I'm going to make me a Charlie Special!" he announced, suddenly inspired by all the sandwich makings.

Taking a slice of whole wheat bread, he pasted on a thick layer of peanut butter. Over this he crumbled a handful of potato chips and topped those with a slice of the bologna.

"Now, for the cover," Charlie said, putting cheese spread on a slice of the raisin bread.

"Hey, you forgot the cookies!" Mike said as Charlie set the raisin bread and cheese on top of his creation.

Charlie shook his head. "Enough is enough," he said. "I'm saving them for dessert."

Ben, Mike, and Doug watched as Charlie took the first bite.

"It's pretty good," he decided aloud. "Try it!"

"No, thanks," the three said together.

Mike and Doug each settled for a peanut butter sandwich. Ben, with a little spirit of adventure, had bologna and cheese.

They all had another round of sandwiches, but this time Charlie had just plain peanut butter. There was something about the peanut butter and bologna together on the Charlie Special that didn't call for a second one.

The boys finished the bag of potato chips, and the last of the bologna disappeared bit by bit, mostly in the direction of Red who had been standing by, waiting for a handout.

"Milk sure would taste good with these," Mike said wistfully, as they started on the cookies.

"Guess we could go home and get some," Ben suggested reluctantly.

They all decided that going home now just to get some milk would spoil everything.

"Water's okay," Mike said, taking a swig from the jug. "I just want to stay here by our own clubhouse, eating our own supper all by ourselves."

"Me, too," Ben and Doug said. Charlie nodded. That was exactly the way he felt.

Supper over, the boys sat in a row on the porch of the clubhouse that had served as their table. This was a better place to sit than on the grass, which the ants seemed to think was their private territory. They were not above biting their own special stinging bite if anybody sat there very long.

Ben reached down, selected a long blade of grass, put it between his hands and blew, making a harsh whistle. The other boys did the same, and for a while they all sat contentedly and noisily whistling through their blades of grass. One whistle was all it took to bring some grown-up to shush them if they tried this in their own yards. Here, they could whistle to their hearts' content.

When they had got the whistling out of their systems, they did some whittling. Nobody made anything but sharpened sticks, which wasn't very interesting until Mike got the idea of using them for pencils.

"Let's play Old Cat." He leaned over and made a ticktacktoe grid in the patch of bare ground in front of him. Square in the center he placed an *X*.

They had an Old Cat tournament which ended rather quickly with the old cat winning.

Then Mike remembered another game that somebody besides the old cat could win.

"I don't know what you call this, but it's fun," he said, making rows of neatly aligned dots on the patch of bare ground.

Taking turns, each boy connected two dots with a line at random all over the playing area Mike had marked out. After a lot of line making, Ben was the first one to draw a line that completed a square, which meant that he had scored a point. He marked a *B* for Ben in the square.

After a long time all the dots were connected, leaving a checkerboard pattern with a *B*, *M*, *D*, or *C* marked in each square.

When they counted them all, there were more *M*'s than any other letter. Twelve, all together. That made Mike the winner of that game.

"Just goes to prove that I'm the smartest," Mike bragged jokingly.

"Okay, if you're so smart," Doug challenged, "then you can figure out how to fix the tilt of the clubhouse!"

"Well, I'm not a genius, just smart," Mike tossed back.

The four sat idly scratching in the dirt with their sticks when Mike said suddenly, "Do you suppose if we all stood together on the high side of the clubhouse and jumped up and down it would make that side go down deeper and level it off?"

The others shrugged.

"Well, we could try it, couldn't we?" Mike insisted when nobody said anything. "Come on!"

They all followed Mike into the clubhouse. Each of them took a place along the north wall of the clubhouse, and when Mike said "jump" they jumped together. Nothing happened.

"Maybe if we all stand in one corner and jump," Mike suggested.

So they tried one corner, and then the other, but still nothing happened, except that everybody was dripping sweat because it was still terribly hot inside the clubhouse.

"If we go outside and lift up on the high side, maybe we could straighten it," Doug suggested.

"Seems to me it'd do more good to raise it from the low side," Ben said as they crawled out from under the clubhouse.

They tried lifting both the high side and the low side of the clubhouse, just to make everybody happy. It was so heavy, however, that they weren't able to budge it an inch.

"We'll figure out something," Charlie said, although at the moment he had no idea what. He hadn't really set his brain to work on that problem, yet.

They sat down again on the porch, their backs against the wall of the clubhouse. Ben picked up the water jug, took a swig, and passed it along. Doug, at the end of the line, hesitated.

"Aw, they're clean germs, Doug," Ben teased. "If you don't take a drink, you'll die of thirst before morning."

"No, thanks. I'm not that thirsty yet," Doug said, sending the jug back down the line. Charlie, Mike, and Ben each took another drink before Ben replaced the cap and set the jug under the clubhouse.

"What else we need to figure out," Charlie said, "is how to get us a good roof."

"If we could earn some money, we could buy the stuff," Mike said.

"Yeah, but how can we earn any money?" Ben asked. "Nobody hires kids except for paper routes, and they're all taken."

"Maybe we could start a fund," Mike suggested. "You know—save our allowances and put the money together."

"With the allowances we get, we'd be old men with long gray beards before we'd have enough," Doug told him.

Chapter Fifteen
In the Clubhouse

When the sun had finally disappeared with a glow of red, the temperature became a bit more comfortable. The boys lolled on the porch of the clubhouse and enjoyed the little breeze that was beginning to stir. From the trees overhead surged a loud, harsh buzzing. Locusts, Uncle Nate said, made that sound, though Charlie had never caught one at it. Closer at hand came the occasional annoying hum of a mosquito followed by a slap as somebody brought it down—or tried to.

Although nobody was really sleepy when it had grown completely dark, it felt like time to go to bed.

Inside the clubhouse, the boys pushed the chair and the building scraps into one corner, propped Doug's flashlight up on the chair and spread out their bed rolls, avoiding the floor ridges as well as they could.

Red wandered about, sniffing each bed roll.

"He's wondering which is his," Mike said.

"Come on, watch dog, you can sleep with me," Charlie invited.

Some Summer!

"No, me!"

"Me!"

"Here, Red!"

After a great deal of consideration, during which time the boys had taken off their sneakers, switched off the flashlight and crawled into their beds, Red finally plunked himself down beside Charlie and snuggled up close.

"Ugh! Sleeping with Red is like sleeping with a hairy hot-water bottle," Charlie declared, trying unsuccessfully to put a little distance between himself and the dog. Every time he edged away, Red snuggled closer.

"You're a good dog, anyway," Charlie said, deciding he was stuck with the persistent hot-water bottle for the night.

The boys were just beginning to settle down after a few complaints about the heat, the mosquitoes, and the hardness of the floor when there was a scuffling sound in Mike's corner.

"I've got to turn around the other way," he said. "The way this floor slants, I feel like I'm standing on my head."

"We've got to figure out some way to fix that," Doug said.

"Yeah," Ben agreed, "trouble is, Aunt Essie keeps us so busy, we don't have time."

"It's lucky we even got the clubhouse built at all," Charlie added grumpily.

"I'm glad she's not our aunt!" Doug said.

"We'd be glad to share her with you!" Charlie offered.

"No thanks!"

"Or you can even have her for your very own—garden and all!" Ben said.

"Yuk!" the Grandys responded together.

"You know, there's something I don't understand," Ben said.

"What's that?" the others wanted to know.

"Remember in Bible School this week we talked about how God wants us to be kind and forgiving to people," Ben said, "and . . . and . . . what's that word? Tenderhearted? Well, we're not mean to Aunt Essie, we do what she tells us to, and we don't sass her—"

"Mom would get after us if we did!" Charlie interrupted.

"Yeah," Ben agreed, "but I sure can't feel tender-hearted toward Aunt Essie. She doesn't need anybody to feel tenderhearted toward her anyway. She can look after herself, I'd say!"

"That's for sure!" Charlie said. "And I don't see how I could ever forgive her for coming and ruining our whole summer!"

"I don't think I'd like her even if she hadn't made us work in the garden. She gets under my skin just because she's her," Ben said. "Do you have to forgive people just for being themselves?"

Charlie sighed. "Beats me! Mr. Hopkins is a nice guy and I liked him for a teacher, but he sure dug up a lot of stuff that I can't figure out."

"Like what else?" This came from Doug's corner.

"Like, how do you know God is real?" Charlie said. "He asked that the very first day."

"Yeah, when I think about that I feel like I'm standing by a great big empty space and don't know if I want to jump in, or if I'm afraid to," Mike said.

There was a long silence. Charlie looked at the night sky that seemed closer than usual through the opening at the top of the clubhouse walls. There was a small sliver of moon with a misty circle around it and hundreds of stars—how many thousands of miles away? And beyond that? Heaven and God Himself? Yet, the Bible said that God was everywhere, so He was right here, too. But how did you know, really, for yourself? Uncle Nate had talked about reading the Bible and praying and meditating on what God said. And he had talked about the Holy Spirit being a witness that God was real. Charlie had heard of people being witnesses, but he'd never thought about the Holy Spirit being a witness. Charlie wasn't sure he knew what it all meant.

Finally, Ben, as though he had been thinking Charlie's thoughts, said in a hushed voice, "It's kind of like with our dad. Sure, I know he was a real person. Mom has told us about him, and we have pictures of him, and things he gave us. But I don't really remember him myself because he died when I was so little. It doesn't seem like he was a real person to me."

Charlie knew exactly how Ben felt. Except for one very special time. Charlie would have liked to tell Ben about it. However, there were some things mixed up in it, and Charlie wasn't ready to talk about it with anybody, not even Ben.

It had happened one day last winter as Charlie was rummaging in the little attic storage space that opened from his and Ben's room. In a box of keepsakes that had belonged to his father as a boy was a small, rather worn Bible. Charlie himself had one almost like it that Uncle Nate had given him, except that Charlie's was like new.

Inside the front cover of the little book Charlie discovered a shiny gold seal with a Bible verse printed on it.

Know thou the God of thy father, and serve him with a perfect heart and with a willing mind: if thou seek him, he will be found of thee.
—I Chronicles 28:9

Below the seal in a scrawl startlingly like Charlie's own handwriting was another Bible verse, beneath which was his father's signature, Robert Charles Scott.

For the first time that Charlie could remember, his father suddenly became a real person—a man who had once been a boy like Charlie himself. Probably his teachers had written on the top of his papers, "Penmanship needs improving," as Charlie's teachers did.

"O God, thou art my God; early will I seek thee," Charlie's father had written long ago and then signed his name. It was more than just a copy of a Bible verse, Charlie felt. It was important business with God—a prayer, a response to the words on the gold seal.

Charlie had sat cross-legged on the floor for a long time lost in thought, one finger absently tracing the edges of the gold seal.

It was a good thing his father had done, he had thought. Stepping to the table-desk and taking his own Bible from the drawer, he had copied inside the front cover, "O God, thou art my God; early will I seek thee," and then he had signed his whole name, Charles Robert Scott.

Then he had heard Ben coming up the stairs. For some reason which he couldn't explain, Charlie had stuffed the two little Bibles into the drawer.

And that was the end of that.

Now as he lay on the old quilt on the floor of the clubhouse, it seemed that he had put the important business with God in the drawer, too. It was as though God, like Charlie's father, had died before Charlie ever got to know Him.

Except, Charlie thought, maybe he did start to answer that prayer way back then. Maybe He's made all this happen because He *wants* me to find out how to know God all for myself. Would God do all that for me?

If my dad were alive, I'd talk with him, Charlie said to himself, but I hardly ever talk to God. No, *never* would be more like it. Not even a "Now I lay me down to sleep" like I used to say when I was a little kid.

But there was more to it than that. It was like Mike had said a while ago. There was this big empty space. Did he want to jump into it, or was he afraid to?

Well, both! He wanted to know God . . . . The trouble was, he had a feeling that knowing Him would involve some changes in himself. And changes were sometimes uncomfortable.

There was the matter of Aunt Essie and being kind, tenderhearted, and forgiving. I don't want to be kind and tenderhearted and forgiving toward Aunt Essie, Charlie thought stubbornly. She never gave us a chance. She just bosses us around and ignores us and doesn't like kids.

Then he remembered something. Didn't the Bible say that Jesus came so that people could know God and live to please Him? And didn't the Bible say, too, that God helps a person *want* to do the good things he should do, and then He helps him do them? If that was the way it was. . . .

Suddenly everything began to fit—all the pieces of the puzzle Charlie had been unwillingly collecting this week. If the not wanting to be kind, tenderhearted, and forgiving got changed to wanting to, wouldn't that be God who did it?

That was how you knew that God is real!

"Lord," Charlie prayed, feeling rather rusty at that sort of thing, "I want to know for myself that You're real. I guess You know what I mean. So do what You have to do. I'm leaving it up to You—about Aunt Essie, You know."

And, having made the jump into the empty space, he finally fell asleep.

The next thing Charlie knew, somebody was dribbling water on his head. Or was it . . . .

"Rain!" said a sleepy voice that was so muffled by the sound of rain beating down on the canvas overhead that Charlie couldn't tell whose it was.

"I'm getting wet!" Doug said in a voice that was not sleepy, but disgusted and loud enough to be heard clearly over the patter of the rain.

Just then there was a splat that sounded as though somebody had thrown a pailful of water into the clubhouse.

"Hey! Who did that!" Doug shouted angrily, having apparently been in the pathway of the flood.

A beam of light came on then, from Doug's corner. Looking overhead, in the light of the flashlight, Charlie saw what had happened. Rain had gathered in a low spot at the edge of the canvas. When it had become heavy enough, it had simply emptied itself over the side and onto Doug's head. Water was now dripping steadily into the clubhouse.

"Let's pull the tarp over the windows before we get any wetter," Ben shouted in order to be heard above the noise of the rain.

The rain was coming down with such force that it seemed to be coming from all directions. The boys struggled with the canvas and finally got it pulled down so that it covered all the window openings.

"That's better!" Doug said, wiping his face with one end of his blanket. Then he rearranged his bedding to make a dry place to sleep and turned off the flashlight.

The clubhouse had a cozy, safe feel now that the rain was shut out, even though it was a little damp inside in spots. Feeling slightly and gloriously chilly for the first time in a long while, Charlie pulled his quilt around himself and Red (who hadn't been the least bit disturbed by the rain) and snuggled underneath.

It was a funny kind of rain, he thought. After being hot and dry for such a long time he would have expected a rip-roaring thunderstorm. This was rip-roaring rain, all right, but only now and then was there a little flash of lightning, followed by a rumble of thunder far off in the distance. Charlie was glad of that. He wasn't afraid of thunderstorms, really, but he didn't like them. In a really bad one, he'd rather be inside a house.

The rain made too much noise for conversation, although Charlie was aware of sounds of discontent from Doug's corner. Finally, however, there was only the slashing of the rain against the tarp.

Just before he fell back to sleep, he remembered something. Had it happened yet, he wondered. Had God changed his feelings toward Aunt Essie?

Charlie thought about Aunt Essie. Do I feel like being forgiving and kind and tenderhearted to her now, he asked himself. No, to be perfectly honest, he did not. He still definitely didn't even want to feel like it.

Maybe this was like one time when he was six and had put a baby tooth that he had pulled out under his pillow to be exchanged for a dime by the Tooth Fairy. His mother, the Tooth Fairy, was sometimes forgetful, and this was one of those times. When he had looked under his pillow, the tooth was still there. And no dime. He had reminded the Tooth Fairy at breakfast and again at bedtime, for good measure. The next morning the tooth was gone and in its place were *two* shiny dimes!

God didn't forget, did He? No, Charlie was sure He didn't. Just the same, it wouldn't hurt to remind Him. Or maybe God was waiting to see if Charlie really meant business.

"I really do mean it," Charlie prayed. "You know how I don't even want to like Aunt Essie. And I don't see how I can change that myself. But the Bible says that anything is possible with You."

The rain beat incessantly on the tarp overhead, and finally, in the monotony of it, Charlie went back to sleep.

Chapter Sixteen
Decorating

When Charlie woke, the rain had stopped. It was still rather dark inside the clubhouse because of the tarp covering the window openings, but he could tell it was morning. Light seeped through the cracks in the walls of the clubhouse, and somebody was nuzzling his arm with a cold, wet nose.

"Go away, Red," he muttered sleepily, pushing the dog away.

Red obligingly turned to Ben, then Doug, and Mike, nuzzling each boy in turn and getting the same reception each time. Then he came back to Charlie, whined and wagged his tail expectantly.

"Okay. You want out. Just a minute." Charlie pushed himself into a sitting position, stretched and yawned, and then lifted the trap door.

Looking into the opening in the dim light, Charlie couldn't believe what he saw. "Will you look at that!" he exclaimed.

Instantly the other boys came to peer over his shoulder.

"Huh!" they exclaimed in one voice, for there was no longer space in the trap door opening for crawling out from under the clubhouse. There was only dirt. Slightly muddy dirt.

"The clubhouse must be sitting flat on the ground!" Charlie declared in wonder as the fact finally became clear to him.

"You don't really want to go out, do you?" Charlie asked Red who, like the boys, was looking down into the hole that was no longer a hole.

"You never know about him," Ben said. "Maybe it's urgent, or maybe he just wants to chase rabbits."

"Well, *I* want to go out," Mike said positively, "and I don't want to chase rabbits!"

"Guess we can get out over the top," Ben suggested.

"Yeah, then we can see what happened and maybe figure out some way to fix it," Doug said.

Since getting ready for bed last night had involved only taking off their sneakers, the boys were quickly ready to face the outside morning world by putting them on again.

This done, Ben leaned a short piece of two-by-four against the wall to use as a toehold and climbed over the wall first, folding the tarp back from the window opening. Charlie handed Red to him, then he, Mike, and Doug climbed over the same way Ben had.

Although nobody had a watch, they could tell it was still very early. The sun was only just beginning to come up. The air had a freshly washed smell to it and everything looked shiny-clean after the night's rain. The trees still dripped, and there were puddles in every little depression in the ground.

The boys walked all around the clubhouse in amazement. It really was sitting flat on the ground!

"No more Leaning Tower of Pisa," Doug said.

Charlie braced himself for another Leaning Tower of Pizza joke, but Doug didn't say any more about that.

"Must be all that rain that did it," Ben said.

"Softened up the ground too much," Charlie added.

"Well, it was a good idea while it lasted," Mike said a little sadly.

"At least now we don't have to figure out how to straighten it," Doug said, "but what are we going to do for a door?"

"What are we going to do for breakfast? We can figure out about a door later. I'm hungry," Mike said.

"Me, too," Ben said. "Guess we'll have to go home. We ate everything we brought with us last night, you know."

"Shucks! Then our camp out will be all over," Mike objected. "Wish we'd thought to bring more food."

"I know where we can get something to eat," Ben said.

"Where?" Mike asked.

"In the garden," Ben replied.

"The garden!" Charlie, Mike, and Doug repeated.

"What's there to eat in the garden for breakfast?" Charlie asked.

"Well, there are tomatoes, anyway. I wouldn't mind a tomato for breakfast once," Ben said.

"I'm hungry enough to eat anything. Let's go get some tomatoes," Mike said, and then added, "but won't Aunt Essie care?"

"Naw, there are lots of them. Besides, it's our garden, too, you know," Ben assured him.

The garden was muddy from the night's downpour, and the tomatoes on the lower parts of the plants were well splashed with mud. However, with a little hunting the boys were able to find ripe tomatoes as clean as though Aunt Essie herself had just washed them.

"Tomatoes aren't too bad for breakfast," Mike declared as he finished his third one. "What else have you got?"

"There's lettuce," Ben suggested.

"Or how about a nice cucumber?" Charlie offered, picking a tiny one and handing it to Mike.

"Not bad," Mike decided, polishing it off in two bites and helping himself to another.

They each had some cucumbers, a little lettuce— it was hard to find much that wasn't muddy—and rounded the meal off with more tomatoes.

"Now I feel like a rabbit," Charlie declared when he had finished his last tomato. "Do rabbits eat tomatoes, though?"

"Speaking of rabbits, where's Red?" Ben wondered.

"Probably off chasing some," Charlie said.

"Guess we'd better go find him. Mom doesn't like it when we let him run in the neighbors' yards," Ben said.

Fortunately, Red was only next door at the Staffords sniffing around their garbage cans, and that gave Charlie an idea.

"Let's take a ride downtown and look in the trash behind the stores just for fun," he suggested.

Everybody thought that was a good idea. The only trouble was, Ben reminded Charlie, they'd have to go in the house to sign out and maybe wake up somebody.

"Aw, your mom wouldn't even know you went," Doug said.

That was probably true, Ben and Charlie agreed, but the rule was that anytime they left the yard they were to sign out.

"I know!" Mike said. "You can sign out back at the clubhouse. If your mother was looking for you that's where she'd expect you to be anyway. So you can just scratch a message in the dirt—mud—and you're all set."

For so early in the morning, that was a pretty good idea, Charlie thought.

They all tramped back to the clubhouse, and Ben signed out in a patch of mud right in front of the clubhouse where anybody could plainly see it in case they should come looking for the four campers. "Gone to town," he printed as neatly as anyone could print in a patch of mud. Then everybody scratched in his first initial.

The trip downtown proved to be the most profitable of any Charlie had made for a long time.

They had gone the rounds of the stores on the north side of the street first and found nothing of interest, not even at Folsom's Hardware. On the other side of the street, however, at the drugstore, right on top of the trash box were three cans of spray paint. One was red, one blue, and one white. The cans were quite full, too. What a find!

Without even bothering to look in the trash behind the grocery store, which rarely if ever had anything interesting in it anyway, the boys made a beeline for the clubhouse.

Nobody had thought about it before, but paint was just what they needed to spruce up the inside of the clubhouse. And now they had some!

Charlie, first over the wall of the clubhouse, took the cap off the can of red paint which he happened to be carrying. He shook it hard until the little ball inside rattled freely, as he had seen Mr. Gage do when he used spray paint. Then he aimed it at the wall and pushed the button on top.

With a hissing sound a spatter of red appeared on the wall.

"Ha! Freckles!" Mike exclaimed, although the freckles turned to a solid blob of color surrounded by only a spatter of freckles as Charlie continued to spray.

Taking turns with the cans of paint (although Charlie found it a little hard to part with a can, once he got going) the boys decorated the walls of the clubhouse with red, white, and blue blobs.

"Neat!"

The only trouble was, Doug pointed out, the green chair didn't look very good with the red, white, and blue walls.

"Well, we can fix that," Mike said, and immediately he sprayed the chair with the can of white paint which he happened to have in his hand at the moment.

That would have been all very well, except that before Mike had finished, the white paint was used up and some of the green showed through.

"How about a blue and white striped chair?" Charlie asked, and began making stripes to cover the green with blue paint. By the time he had finished the stripes, the can of blue paint was practically empty. He took the can of red paint from Ben.

"On second thought, how about a red, white, and blue checkered chair?" he asked as he began to spray red stripes crosswise over the white and blue.

Now that was *really* nifty, everybody agreed when Charlie had finished.

Chapter Seventeen
Pickles

"Today we begin making pickles!" Aunt Essie announced brightly at the breakfast table the Monday morning after the camp out.

If Charlie hadn't heard the words, he might have thought from her tone of voice that she had said something like, "One of the trees in the back yard is just full of dollar bills this morning; so we'll pick them by the bushel and have a good time spending them!"

Of course, that wasn't what she said.

Had Aunt Essie made such an announcement last week, Charlie would have been so filled with anger that he probably would have exploded right then and there. He didn't even like pickles. Not any kind. Cucumbers hadn't tasted so bad right from the garden Saturday morning for breakfast, but that was different.

In spite of everything, surprisingly, Charlie discovered that he really didn't feel terribly upset about the prospect of pickle-making. Way down deep inside him, he thought something was actually changing. Almost, he thought, he could feel kind toward Aunt Essie.

At Aunt Essie's request, Ben and Charlie brought up from the basement six brown-and-tan earthenware crocks of different sizes. These were what she had always used for making her award-winning pickles years ago, she explained. One couldn't make pickles without earthenware crocks.

Ben and Charlie didn't bother to mention that earthenware crocks were also good for housing frogs and tadpoles. In fact, only last summer the largest one had been the home of Freddy the Frog whom they had raised from a tadpole. Freddy, however, had hopped out one night and hadn't been heard from since.

"Wonder what ever happened to ol' Freddy?" Charlie mused as they made the second trip down the basement stairs.

"Probably went to live with his relatives in Elwood's swamp where we got him in the first place," Ben said.

"Yeah, I guess," Charlie said. They had discussed the matter many times and had always come to the same conclusion.

"Probably still there, happy as a frog," Ben said cheerfully.

"Yeah, I guess," Charlie said again, "but it makes me feel sort of sad to think of his crock being used for pickles, even 'award-winning' pickles."

When Aunt Essie had thoroughly scrubbed the crocks, the boys carried them back to the basement and set them in a row beside the stairway. This was where the cucumbers would be turned into pickles. Pickles, it seemed, needed to be kept as cool as possible.

Ben and Charlie helped Aunt Essie pick and wash the sticky, green, prickly cucumbers.

Then they made a horrible discovery. They had thought Aunt Essie had said, "*Today* we make pickles." What she had actually said was, "Today we *begin* making pickles." One didn't make pickles in a day. At least Aunt Essie didn't.

"These will be nine-day pickles," she said, half to herself, as she emptied a bowl of cut-up cucumbers into one of the crocks.

This time Ben did give an answer, although she probably hadn't expected one. "Nine days to make a pickle!" He exclaimed in disbelief.

"It takes even longer than that to make dills!" Aunt Essie said enthusiastically. "I have my own special, no-fail recipe for those. The one that always used to get me the blue ribbon at the country fair. Why, the way the cucumbers are coming on, we'll be making pickles the rest of the summer!"

She was using the "money tree" tone of voice again, but the words sounded more like a jail sentence. Pickles the rest of the summer! Charlie wasn't sure if even God could make him not mind about that! But suddenly he realized that Aunt Essie had actually talked to Ben— honestly answered him, anyway.

Monday afternoon, pickle-making chores finished for the day, Doug and Mike came over, and the gang retreated to the clubhouse.

"You know, I kinda like it better like this," Mike said as they scrambled over the wall and into the clubhouse. "I got tired of getting down on my hands and knees to get inside all the time."

"You've got something there. Only I don't think I'm going to want to crawl over the top all the time, either," Ben said.

"We could put in a regular doorway, maybe," Charlie suggested.

"That would take some sawing," Doug objected. "Can you imagine cutting a doorway in the wall with the rusty old saw?"

"It'd be easier to chew one through with our teeth, like beavers," Mike said, making exaggerated chewing motions and sounds.

"I've got an idea!" Charlie said suddenly.

"Does it use a saw?" Mike wanted to know.

"Nope," Charlie said. "Only trouble is, we'd have to take off one whole wall and then put it back again."

The other boys made protesting noises, but they finally stopped and listened to Charlie's idea.

"Like I said, we take off one wall, then we nail a board on this way," Charlie explained, making up and down motions with his hand. "That'll be one side of the doorway. The other will be the cornerpost, you know. Then we nail the wall boards back on. Of course, the boards on that side will stick out on the other corner, but what will that matter?"

The others shrugged.

"Guess that'd be okay," Ben said.

"Then we've got to have a door," Doug reminded.

"Maybe we could nail together a couple of pieces of that plywood you guys got from Hutchinson's," Charlie suggested, knowing they didn't have one piece big enough.

"Let's get to work then!" Mike said.

First, they had to decide on which side of the clubhouse to put the door. They finally settled on the west side, the same side the trap door had been on, since they were used to going in on that side anyway.

Taking off one wall proved to be a not-too-difficult task, and by suppertime that was done. The problem of finding a board long enough to nail on vertically for one side of the doorway would have to wait until later.

On Tuesday afternoon, after pickle-making chores, the boys tackled the task of making a door, since that seemed to be the next logical step.

As Charlie observed, "If we don't make the door first, we might make the doorway the wrong size and then we'd be in trouble."

There were two good-sized pieces of plywood that Doug and Mike had salvaged from the Hutchinson's that day so long ago when Ben and Charlie had to plant the garden. These they nailed together with a smaller piece of plywood on each side for strength.

"There!" Ben said, standing the new door on end when they had finished. "It's nothing fancy, but it'll do!"

There were absolutely no pieces of wood left that were long enough to use for the side of the doorway.

"Maybe we could use the middle roof board," Charlie suggested hesitantly, knowing that three roof boards were already few enough. That seemed to be the only board in the whole clubhouse that could possibly be spared, if one must be spared.

After some discussion, the boys decided that as long as it didn't rain too hard, two roof boards would hold up the tarp. Maybe something—somehow, sometime—could be found for a proper roof. So, in the end, the middle roof board became one side of the doorway.

As the week progressed, Ben and Charlie found that the making of pickles wasn't quite so bad as it had sounded when they had first discovered how long it took. True, almost every day there were cucumbers to be picked and washed. And there were trips to the store for bags of coarse pickling salt and spices with strange-sounding names like *turmeric* and *tarragon*. What happened to the cucumbers to make them into pickles, Aunt Essie trusted to no one but herself, which, of course, was fine with Ben and Charlie.

It was rather interesting, in a mild sort of way— Charlie thought—the cucumbers sitting for days and days in the salty water (brine, Aunt Essie called it) and vinegar, and only Aunt Essie knew what else. It was almost as though there were something alive down there in the mysterious deeps of the crocks. Aunt Essie had to put plates weighted down with jars of water on top of the cucumbers to keep them under the brine.

"I think the cucumbers want out," Ben joked as he and Charlie went past the row of crocks on an errand to the basement.

"Maybe they don't want to be pickles," Charlie said. "Do you think if we took 'em outdoors and took off the plates and jars of water they'd escape like Freddy did?"

The boys snickered all the way up the stairs at the thought of Aunt Essie's dill pickles disappearing in the night.

And then, there was the smell of pickle making— the pungent aroma of vinegar with spices tied up in a little cloth bag heating on the stove. If you breathed in the steam, it made your eyes water and almost took your breath away. Charlie had tried it. It was a good smell, he thought, even though he didn't care for pickles.

By Friday afternoon the clubhouse remodeling job was done. The new door swung readily open and shut on the hinges that had been on the trap door. The trap door itself was now nailed solidly shut, a part of the floor, which had almost the appearance of a patchwork quilt with the floor boards running in two directions and the trap door rectangle in one corner.

"Just one problem," Doug said as the gang rested from their labors.

Charlie thought he knew what Doug's problem was. "The door won't stay shut tight, right?" he asked.

Doug nodded. "A little wind could blow it open."

"I've got just the thing to fix that in my culch pile," Charlie said. "Come on, there might be some other stuff we could use, too."

The culch pile yielded not only an old screen-door spring to keep the door tightly closed but also a handle to put on the outside to make it easier to open. And, happily, there were some screws of the right size for installing both the spring and the handle.

"Charlie," Mike declared as the boys tromped up the basement stairs, "your culch pile is almost as good as Folsom's Hardware! Too bad there isn't a roof for the clubhouse in there."

The cucumbers kept coming and coming. It seemed that for every one they picked, three grew in its place. It was a bumper crop, Aunt Essie said. She was making the smaller ones into bread-and-butter pickles and the larger ones into dills.

"We'll still be picking cucumbers at Christmas time," Charlie said one morning as he and Ben were in the garden picking cucumbers for the tenth day in a row, not counting Sunday.

"It's like that Bible story where the poor widow lady kept pouring out oil from a jug that was supposed to be empty," Ben said.

"Yeah, the oil never did stop coming until all the jars she had and all she could borrow from her neighbors were filled to the brim," Charlie said. "There's still an awful lot of empty jars in our basement. I sure hope the neighbors don't have any for us to borrow!"

Besides the cucumbers, there were tomatoes hanging red, ripe, and bountiful on the vines. Just begging to be canned, Aunt Essie said. Of course, it was also Ben and Charlie's job to help with those.

Tomatoes, though, weren't all that bad. Peeling them turned out to be so interesting that Mike and even Doug begged to help. When Aunt Essie poured boiling water over the tomatoes, the skins could be easily pulled off. It was more like helping them off with their jackets than peeling them, Charlie thought.

In spite of the extra work of pickle making and tomato canning, Charlie discovered that something really had changed in the way he felt about Aunt Essie and the garden work. Even Ben noticed.

"How come you're not acting mad anymore when we have to do something for Aunt Essie?" he asked one afternoon as the two of them headed for town on an errand for Aunt Essie.

At first Charlie didn't think he could talk about it with anybody, not even Ben. But then he blurted out, "It's God!"

"Huh?" Ben responded.

"That's what it is, or I mean who it is," Charlie said. Then he went on to tell Ben about the things he had thought about the night of the camp out. "And now I'm beginning to understand about how you know God is real," he finished. "If you ignore Him, it's easy to be afraid He's not real, but if you ask Him to make you believe that He's real, pretty soon you start to understand Him better."

Ben was quiet for about half a block. Finally, just before they reached the grocery store, he said, "That's good! That's really good, Charlie!"

That night at bedtime Charlie got out the little Bible that had belonged to their father and showed it to Ben.

"This was Dad's, huh?" Ben said in a hushed voice, taking it from Charlie and turning it over and over.

"Yeah," Charlie said softly, "and let me show you something." He took the little book from Ben and opened the front cover. "Look."

"Looks like your writing, Charlie."

"No, he wrote it."

"Dad wrote that . . . when he was a kid like us," Ben said wonderingly, running his finger reverently over the writing. " 'O God, thou art my God; early will I seek thee,' " he read aloud slowly. "That was a good thing to write, wasn't it?"

"I copied it in my Bible and signed my name like he did," Charlie said. "Sometimes when I'm alone I read it, too, especially John 1. I think it's my favorite chapter now." Then he crawled into bed feeling very good about finally sharing everything with Ben.

Chapter Eighteen
Plans for a Roof

At last the day came that Ben and Charlie had been looking forward to all summer. The morning bus chugged away from the drugstore corner and headed down Main Street toward the highway. Aunt Essie was on her way back to Florida.

The boys silently watched the bus out of sight. Then Charlie, suddenly feeling like a kite cut free from its string, gave a yell and headed up the street running.

"Beat you home!" he called to Ben, who still stood on the sidewalk looking down the street.

Minutes later, panting and laughing, they jostled each other through the back door and into the house.

In the middle of the kitchen they stopped and let out a wild Indian war whoop.

"Halloooo, nobody!" Ben shouted.

"Hello, yourself!" somebody answered from outside.

"Hey, you guys, come on in," Charlie called, seeing Doug and Mike at the back door.

"Is she gone?" Mike asked in a stage whisper as he walked in the door followed by Doug.

"You don't think we'd be acting like this if she was still here, do you?" Ben answered.

"Nothing left of her but sixty-seven hundred jars of pickles and canned tomatoes!" Charlie said. Then, after a moment's pause, he added, "You know, it's going to seem kind of funny without her. She was a pretty nice old lady after all. She just didn't know much about kids. But I think she finally did get used to us."

"I'll miss her cookies," Mike said wistfully. "She didn't leave any, did she?"

"Later, you chowhound," Doug said to his brother. "Did you forget what we came for?"

Mike brightened. "Oh, yeah! Come on, you guys. We want to show you something."

"What?" Ben and Charlie wanted to know.

"Don't ask questions. Just come on!" Doug insisted.

The boys took off on their bikes with Doug in the lead. Down Main Street they went, past the stores, then left onto Locust Street. They stopped in front of a neat little gray and white house where a carpenter was building a porch on the side. Beside the front door were three fancy iron posts, some lumber, and several large panels of white fiberglass. A *For Sale* sign was taped to one of the panels.

Charlie was off his bike and inspecting the items for sale almost before the other boys had their feet on the ground.

"These would make a neat roof!" he said, running his hands across the ribbed surface of one of the panels.

"That's what we thought," Doug said. "We had to come down here this morning for some stuff Mom wanted from the lady who lives here. That's how we happened to see it. We could just nail it on top of the clubhouse, and we wouldn't need any more lumber or anything."

"It would let some light in, too," Mike said, holding up a piece of the fiberglass.

"How much do they want for it?" Ben asked practically.

"A dollar and a half a piece," Doug said, as though dollars grew as bountifully as the cucumbers in Aunt Essie's garden.

"A dollar and a half!" Ben exclaimed. "We'd need maybe four pieces . . . ." His voice drifted off as he stooped and made some scratchings with a twig in a bare spot of ground. "Six dollars for four!" he said. Ben's dollars didn't grow like cucumbers.

"Maybe we could figure out some way to earn the money," Doug said.

"Maybe," Ben said with a small amount of hope in his voice. "We could at least figure out for sure how many pieces we'd need so we'd know exactly how much it would cost."

It took a trip to the clubhouse, back to Locust Street, then back to the clubhouse again, to figure out, with the help of Charlie's six foot two-inch measure, that they would need five panels of the fiberglass to make a roof for the clubhouse.

"Seven dollars and fifty cents!" Ben said, sitting down in a discouraged lump on the grass beside the clubhouse.

"It might as well be seven hundred dollars and don't bother about the fifty cents," Charlie said, joining Ben on the grass. He knew that between the four of them they had less than enough for one panel of fiberglass.

Mike and Doug sat on the porch of the clubhouse beside the door, elbows on their knees, chins resting on their hands.

"There must be some way we could earn money," Doug said in a determined voice.

"Hey!" Ben said suddenly. "How about selling garden stuff. Tomatoes, maybe. There's still plenty of those left."

"Yeah!" Charlie, Doug, and Mike all said together in a balloon of excitement that was quickly deflated by Ben's next words.

"But who would buy 'em?" he said in a discouraged tone. "Everybody's got so many tomatoes, you can't even give 'em away."

"Yeah," the others said again, this time having hit rock bottom.

"I know how we can make forty cents," Mike said jokingly, in an attempt to cheer everybody up.

"Forty cents!" Doug said disdainfully.

"How?" Charlie asked. Sometimes a little can turn out to be more than you expect.

"Ride our bikes in the Country Fair parade next Saturday. They give every kid that's in it a dime, you know," Mike said.

The Country Fair was a yearly event in MacArthur that took place on the Saturday before Labor Day.

"Wow, big deal!" Doug said. "We'll have to do that! Only I think you have to be under ten years old."

"Wait a minute!" Ben said. "There must be something we could do at the Country Fair to make some money."

"Like what?" Mike asked.

"Sell something, maybe? They have all those stands where people sell stuff they've made and things to eat, you know," Ben said.

"But all we've got to sell is tomatoes that nobody wants," Doug reminded him.

"Hey, hey, hey!" Ben said excitedly. "I know something we've got lots of that maybe we could sell!" He looked significantly at Charlie.

"Pickles!" Charlie said. "Aunt Essie's pickles!"

Mike and Doug wrinkled their noses.

"Pickles?" Mike said.

"Who'd want to buy a jar of pickles," Doug asked, "When you can buy 'em at the store?"

Ben shrugged. "People might. They're supposed to be some kind of special pickles. She used to always win prizes. Everybody knows Aunt Essie's a good cook. We could put up a sign, 'Aunt Essie's Pickles.' "

The boys were silent a moment, mulling over the possibility of going into the pickle business. Ben interrupted the silence.

"No," he said, back to rock bottom again. "We can't do that. Mom wouldn't let us get rid of all those jars. We'd have to sell them in jars, of course."

So that was the end of that.

Or was it? Charlie felt an idea coming on way in the back of his head. He pulled his knees up to his chest, folded his arms around them and rocked back and forth. Suddenly he had it!

"I know what we can sell!" he announced, scrambling to his feet. "Come on!"

With the other boys asking questions he wouldn't answer, Charlie led the way to the house and down to the basement. From the rows and rows of filled jars on the shelves in the corner of the basement, Charlie picked out a jar of fat dill pickles. Then, still followed by the others, he went back up the stairs and into the kitchen.

"Somebody open this, please, while I find what I need," he said, handing the jar of pickles to Ben.

From a drawer he took a small paring knife, which he lay on the counter. After quite a bit of rummaging through drawers he found a handful of used, but clean, Popsicle sticks. He had remembered seeing Aunt Essie saving and washing them whenever he and Ben had a Popsicle for a special treat. Aunt Essie didn't believe in throwing away anything useful. Charlie could easily understand that, though he couldn't quite imagine Aunt Essie with a culch pile.

Ben, Doug, and Mike worked at trying to unscrew the lid of the jar of pickles. Finally, they got it off and watched Charlie ease a pickle out of the jar with the help of the paring knife. He shook the juice off the pickle into the jar and made a small slit in the stem end of the pickle with the knife. Then he stuck one of the Popsicle sticks through the slit into the pickle.

"A Pickle Pop!" he announced triumphantly, holding up his new invention.

"Hey, neat!" Mike exclaimed. "Let me try it!" Mike was the only one of the four who cared for pickles.

Charlie handed Mike the Pickle Pop and watched with satisfaction as Mike bit off the end of the pickle. A pickle on a stick looked like a very good way to eat pickles, Charlie thought. If you liked pickles.

Mike, making approving sounds, nibbled away on his Pickle Pop. "Now that's the way to eat a pickle!" he declared when there was nothing left but the stick. "Make me another one, please!"

Charlie fished another pickle from the jar, made a slit with the knife, shoved Mike's stick into that pickle, and handed it to him with a flourish.

"They're really good, no kidding!" Mike said. "They might not take the place of Aunt Essie's cookies, but they're good! Here take a bite." He held the new Pickle Pop toward Doug who took a small nibble.

"Hey! That is good!" Doug said. "Fix me one, too, please, Charlie!"

"Me, too," Ben said. "Looks like they'd be fun to eat, even if I don't like pickles."

So Charlie fixed Pickle Pops for Doug and Ben, and then, because Ben seemed to be enjoying his, he made one for himself.

He took a small exploratory bite from the end of the pickle. Surprisingly, it was almost good. Then, because the juice was running down the stick onto his hand, he licked off the stick and the pickle. It was really not bad at all, Charlie thought as he ate the Pickle Pop, and it was fun to eat, though a little messy, since each bite made more juice run down the stick.

"Maybe I do like pickles, after all," Charlie declared when he had finished. To be perfectly honest, he didn't remember ever trying one before.

Mom came into the kitchen just then, home for lunch. "I never thought I'd hear you say that, Charlie Scott," she said, laughing. "What's going on here, anyway?"

The boys told her about their need to make some money which had led to Charlie's invention. Charlie made his mother a Pickle Pop to try for herself.

"Do you think people would buy 'em if we had a stand at the Country Fair?" Ben asked as his mother approvingly nibbled the Pickle Pop.

"I wouldn't be at all surprised if they did," she said. "Mike and Doug, why don't you see if you can stay for lunch, and we can talk some more about it. Aunt Essie left us a big bowl of kidney bean salad, and there are some chocolate chip cookies in the cookie jar."

While Doug and Mike called home to get permission to stay, Ben and Charlie helped get things on the table for lunch.

As they ate, the boys made plans for the Pickle Pop stand.

Going into business called for spending money before you made any, they soon learned. First of all, there was a fee just for the privilege of having a stand at the Country Fair. That was fifty cents. Then there was the matter of Popsicle sticks. Mom thought they could be bought by the box at Benson's Drug Store.

"You really should have paper napkins, too, since the Pickle Pops get rather juicy," she added.

"Where are we going to get the money for all that stuff?" Ben wailed, and Charlie felt as though the Pickle Pop business had gone broke before it ever began.

Mom said she'd be willing to loan them what they needed, and they could pay her back after the fair.

"What if we don't make enough to pay you back plus the seven-fifty for the fiberglass, too?" Ben wanted to know.

That was a chance you had to take when you went into business, Mom told him. "I don't think you have to worry, though," she added. "A Pickle Pop stand at the Country Fair sounds like a good idea to me."

In the afternoon the boys biked down to Locust Street to see if the owner of the fiberglass panels would consider holding them until after the Country Fair. Between them they had scraped up a dollar to offer as a down payment.

"What if he's already sold the fiberglass?" Mike asked worriedly on the way.

Charlie was anxiously wondering the same thing.

Such a catastrophe hadn't happened. The panels still leaned against the front of the house with the For Sale sign taped to them.

Doug nervously explained their errand to the grouchy-looking owner, who turned out to be not so grouchy as he looked.

"Sure!" the man said. "If you fellows want that fiberglass, I'll be glad to hold it for you until you get the rest of the money. I'll even throw in half a can of sealer. You'll need that to keep your roof from leaking where you join the panels together. I'll show you how to do it."

So that was taken care of. Now all they had to do was sell lots of Pickle Pops.

On Friday the gang gathered together the things they would need for the Pickle Pop stand.

They left the most difficult item—a sign—until last. Doug, who, everybody agreed, did the neatest printing, was elected to make it. First, though, they had to decide what it should say.

"Pickle Pops, of course," Mike said.

"And how much they cost," Ben added.

They had already spent a great deal of time deciding that ten cents would be a fair price. That was how much the grocery store charged for the ones they sold from the big glass jar that sat on top of the meat case. They probably weren't nearly so good as Aunt Essie's, and they didn't come on sticks. People ought to feel that they were getting a bargain on the Pickle Pops.

"We ought to have a slogan," Doug said, like 'Best Pickles in Town.' "

"How about 'Wonderfully Delicious'?" Mike suggested. "Or 'Scrumptious' is a good word."

" 'Good to the Last Lick'?" Ben offered.

"I know! 'Juicy Good!' With an exclamation mark," Mike said.

Juicy good! That had the right sound to it, everybody thought.

"And then we ought to put something like, 'Made from Aunt Essie's Famous Dill Pickles,' " Ben said grandly. "Mom says lots of people in town know how good Aunt Essie makes pickles."

"Okay!" Doug said, and Mike and Charlie nodded approval.

Charlie found a large, heavy, white paper bag in the kitchen drawer and carefully cut a rectangle from it. Doug, using a black felt tip pen, printed "Pickle Pops" in big letters across the top, and underneath, "10 cents." In smaller letters, he wrote, "Juicy Good!" and, finally, below that, "Made from Aunt Essie's Famous Dill Pickles."

It was a good-looking sign, they all thought, when Doug had finished, except that there was a blank space at the bottom.

"We ought to have a picture of a Pickle Pop to fill that space," Doug said, "but I'm no artist."

"Do you think you could draw one, Charlie?" Ben asked.

Charlie couldn't draw just anything, but he thought he could draw a Pickle Pop. He drew one first with a pencil, in case he had to erase, which he didn't. Then he traced over it with the pen.

"Not bad, Charlie!" Doug declared, "but it ought to be colored, don't you guys think?"

Charlie got a collection of colored pencils from his culch pile. He found one exactly the right shade of green for the pickle. For the stick he used light brown.

"Neat, man!" Mike said when Charlie had finished.

They all agreed that it was a very satisfactory sign.

Country Fair, here we come!

Chapter Nineteen
The Fair

Almost too excited to eat, Ben and Charlie hurried through breakfast Saturday morning and were delighted when their mother excused them from helping with the breakfast things so that they could get ready for their big day.

They were just coming up the basement stairs with four extra jars of pickles that they had decided they should take—just in case business was extra good—when Doug and Mike arrived.

Quickly they loaded up and set off for town with Ben and Charlie navigating the wagon and Doug and Mike following behind carrying between them a folding table they had brought from their house.

The place the boys had been assigned for the Pickle Pop stand was in front of Hatcher's Farm and Garden Store, almost at the end of Main Street. Not a very good spot, Charlie thought. On one side was a booth with all kinds of plants for sale. Mrs. Watson from church was running it. On the other, the Maple Ridge Ladies'

Aid had a display of handmade things—knitted and crocheted caps, scarves, mittens, embroidered pictures, and the like.

"Who'd want to buy any of that stuff?" Mike wondered, referring with a sweep of his hands to both the handmade things and the plants.

Charlie wondered, too. He began to worry that nobody would even come down to their end of the street. He felt sure that if people saw the Pickle Pops they would want to buy them. But what if nobody even walked by the stand? Or hardly anybody, anyway? That would be awful! He didn't think he could stand it!

The boys unfolded the table, making sure the legs were securely fastened, and spread the Scotts' red, white, and blue picnic tablecloth over it. On the front they pinned the sign. On the table they set three jars of pickles—one opened with a fork stuck in it, the box of Popsicle sticks, a package of white paper napkins, and an old, gray metal fishing tackle box Charlie had found long ago in somebody's trash. This they would use for a money box. There were more jars of pickles in the wagon, plus a jug of soapy water and a roll of paper towels for washing hands. The water and towels had been Mom's idea.

Nodding with satisfaction, the boys stood back and admired their handiwork.

"Now all we need is some customers," Doug said, rubbing his hands together.

All up and down MacArthur's Main Street were gaily decorated booths and tables selling everything from pottery and jewelry to sloppy joes and apple pie. The spicy-pungent fragrance of apple butter cooking in a kettle over an open fire filled the air. Banjo music blared from a loudspeaker, crowded out now and then by the electrical whine of the tool across the street that carved out signs to order on pieces of wood. Everywhere there were people of all sizes, shapes, and ages. Some faces were familiar, but there were more that were not.

For a long time the boys stood in a row behind the folding table and watched the people passing by. Now and then somebody glanced their way, but nobody stopped to buy a Pickle Pop.

Next door at the Ladies' Aid booth, business was booming. A steady line of customers carried away handmade caps and scarves and embroidered samplers. Even the plant booth appeared to have some business. Everybody else, it seemed, was selling things.

"Probably too early in the morning to eat pickles," Ben said philosophically when Charlie, Doug, and Mike began to worry aloud that they wouldn't sell any Pickle Pops at all.

Finally, two little old ladies who had been browsing at the Ladies' Aid booth next door stopped and looked at the Pickle Pop sign.

"Oh my! Pickle Pops!" one of them exclaimed to the other. "I never heard of Pickle Pops before, did you, Edith?"

"Dear me, no," said the other lady. "Always something new, isn't there? Are those Essie Morgan's dill pickles?" she asked the boys then, pointing to the sign.

"Yes, ma'am," Ben answered in a cheerful, businesslike manner.

"Then I'll have one, please," the second lady said. "Nobody makes dill pickles like Essie Morgan."

"And so will I," said the first lady. "I haven't had Essie's pickles for years, but I remember how good they were."

They watched as Charlie forked two pickles from the jar and poked Popsicle sticks into the ends.

"My! My! What a clever idea!" the first lady exclaimed.

They paid their dimes. Charlie handed them the Pickle Pops, and Ben gave them each a napkin.

"Mmmmm! Every bit as good as I remember!" the first lady said as she took a bite of her Pickle Pop.

"Juicy, but good, just as the sign says!" the other lady agreed as they walked off down the street.

In a few minutes a man with three little girls and a boy stopped.

"There they are, Daddy—those pickles on a stick like those ladies had! I want one!" the biggest girl shouted.

"Me, too!" chorused the other children.

The man bought a Pickle Pop for each of the children and one for himself.

After that there was a steady flow of customers, people who had seen someone else eating a Pickle Pop and wanted to try one for themselves. A few satisfied customers was all it took to get the Pickle Pop business on its feet.

At noon Mrs. Scott and the Grandys, who were all enjoying the fair together, appeared with lunch. It was an extra special meal bought from booths up the street. There were sloppy joes, milk shakes made with homemade ice cream, and watermelon. But Charlie didn't think he would have cared if they had brought only water and a dry crust of bread, he was having such a good time selling Pickle Pops. And just then Uncle Nate and Pastor Danford showed up, eating hot dogs and sauntering along.

"We left some carpet remnants at your clubhouse," Pastor called cheerfully. "It looks pretty nice. You boys did a great job."

The boys were ready to give Pastor a Pickle Pop on the house for his contributions to the clubhouse, but Pastor paid them. Then he and Uncle Nate strolled over to the plant table. Mrs. Danford was working for Mrs. Watson during the lunch hour. She looked a little bit discouraged. Not many people were buying plants. They didn't have as much appeal as pickles.

It was a good thing Ben and Charlie had brought along the extra jars of pickles. By five o'clock when everybody began packing up to get ready for the evening's activities, they had opened the last jar. There was an accumulation of empty jars in the wagon, and the box of Popsicle sticks was almost empty. On the other hand, and best of all, the tackle box had a satisfying collection of coins and dollar bills.

The boys parked the wagon with the leftovers of the day's venture by the Scotts' back door and sat down in a huddle on the sidewalk to count the contents of the tackle box. Red, who had been denied admittance to the fair, raced from one boy to another, tail whipping back and forth, cold nose poking at their hands and at the change.

The metal box scraped its way around the circle as the boys scooped the coins from their separate compartments and began to count.

"Enough to pay back what we owe Mom, buy the fiberglass for the roof, and even some left over!" Ben said triumphantly when they had finished tallying the money.

"Yippee!" they all shouted.

"I have an idea," Charlie said.

The boys glanced at him, expectant. He'd had a string of pretty good ideas this summer.

"Let's use some of the leftover money to buy a plant," he told them. "I don't think it would be that hard to take care of."

Doug and Mike almost fell over backward. Ben looked hard at Charlie for a moment, then said, "Well, if you want to. . . ."

"Sure. The plant table didn't do too well, and, after all, Mrs. Watson's a pretty nice lady, and she had Mrs. Danford helping her. And the Danfords gave us those carpet remnants. We ought to help them out."

"You're right," Doug and Mike agreed.

"We could keep it on the clubhouse porch to spruce it up," Ben added.

They trooped back to the fair. Most of the booths and tables were closing down, but some of the plants were still out. Mrs. Danford was helping Mrs. Watson pack up the red van. They looked up when the boys approached.

Charlie pointed to a thriving little plant in a green pot. It seemed to be all leaves. "What kind of plant is that?" he asked.

"That's a Chinese ivy, Charlie," Mrs. Danford told him.

"How much does it cost?"

"Fifty cents."

"We'd like to buy it, please."

They paid their money and carried the plant back to the clubhouse. Charlie set it on a corner of one of the porches.

"I'll get some water for it," Ben said. He strode away.

Charlie stuck his hand in the dirt of the plant pot. "Too dry!" he exclaimed. "We'll have to get some of that fertilizer we used on the garden," he mused. "Seems like we left a bag of it somewhere."

"Maybe we could sort of have a little garden back here some day," Mike said.

"Sure!" Charlie told him. Then he smiled. God had certainly changed a lot of things.

It had been some summer, Charlie thought, better than he could ever have imagined, in spite of everything. No, it was *because* of everything, he decided, like the time the Tooth Fairy had forgotten to put a dime under his pillow and then had left *two* shiny dimes to make up for it.

"Good ol' Aunt Essie!" Charlie said.